Starlet's Fall

Visit www.booksurge.com to order additional copies.

J.W. MCKENNA

STARLET'S FALL

2008

Starlet's Fall

CHAPTER ONE

Heather slouched on the bus bench, scratching her leg. She was dressed down today and her clothes felt uncomfortable on her. It was funny what one could get used to wearing, she thought, remembering just yesterday she had worn a black mini-skirt and pink tank top—without underwear. Today Heather had on a jean skirt and a designer T-shirt and looked almost respectable as she scanned the line of passengers coming in from out of town on this beautiful day in early June.

It was boring being here, but it was damn sight better than hooking, she mused. She told herself to be grateful for the break because soon she'd be back on the streets fulltime, turning tricks.

Billy often sent his "bottom girl" to the Hollywood bus stop, the prime spot to find new meat, as he liked to say. Heather herself had been one of the innocents who had passed through the dirty bus station four years ago. It seemed like a lifetime now to the twenty-year-old. Heather wasn't even her real name—it had been so long, the name she'd been born with seemed like a stranger to her. Like so many others, she had dreams of being "discovered" before she ran out of money. Ha. What a fucking joke. Yet they never stopped coming—fresh-faced teens from Iowa, Ohio or Alabama, all convinced they'll be the next Cameron Diaz or Lindsey Lohan. What a fucking bunch of idiots!

Many will arrive just as she had been, not running to some dream as much as fleeing a nightmare. Her stepdad had started molesting Heather when she was thirteen. When Heather offered up that as the reason her grades had fallen and her stepdad denied it, her mother refused to believe her. So at sixteen, she had fled west with vague ideas of stardom. She certainly had been pretty enough to make it—and she might've, if her money had not run out less than a week after she had arrived.

Heather sighed and shifted position to watch another door where passengers were filing through. Any girl who takes a bus to Hollywood might as well hang a sign around her neck that says: "I'm nearly broke and desperate!" It was so easy to find new talent for Billy, Heather almost felt guilty.

She spotted a potential candidate at once, a cute sandy-haired teenager coming through the door from the Phoenix bus, a small suitcase banging against her thigh. Heather had to move quickly now, for she knew there were other bottom girls who were always circling. Heather got up and approached the girl. Close up, she had that familiar wide-eyed look, caught between expectation and fear, and Heather immediately pegged her as another runaway. She guessed her age between sixteen and nineteen. She dropped her purse as the girl walked past and cursed as she bent down to scoop up the items that had fallen out. The girl, Heather noted with satisfaction, stopped to help her.

"Thanks!" Heather said brightly. "I'm so clumsy!" She stood up. "You meeting someone here?"

"Uh, no, not really," the girl said. She had on jeans and a dark green Notre Dame T-shirt that fit snugly over her breasts. Heather noted how she must be a solid C-cup at least. She felt a twinge of envy and wondered for a moment if they were real.

Shit, of course they're real, she thought, *the girl hasn't been corrupted by Hollywood yet!*

"Are you?"

"Yeah, I was—but I just got a call to say she missed the bus!" Heather lied smoothly. "My name's Heather. What's yours?"

"I'm Kristy, with a K."

"Well, if you need help with anything, let me know, okay? I've lived here for years." She stepped back, as if she was about to walk away.

Kristy picked up her small suitcase and looked around. "Uh, wait—could you tell me of a good, cheap hotel around here somewhere?"

Heather laughed. "Well, there's good and expensive, or cheap and dirty—which do you want?"

"Well, I guess I'd better take cheap and dirty," she said, grimacing at the thought.

"I know a place that'll do." She checked her watch. "I got time. Come on, I'll take you there if you'd like. It's just a couple blocks away."

"Oh, that'd be great. Thanks."

She led the girl out into the California sunshine. Kristy squinted and averted her eyes. Heather smiled at her reaction. This was going to be too easy, she thought. Girl fresh off the bus, doesn't know shit, can't even stand the bright sunlight. Must be gray all the time back home in Peoria. "Come on, it's this way. Where ya from?"

"Indiana. Evansville."

Heather nodded to herself, thinking, *I was close.* The girls had to dodge around a homeless man who leered at them. Heather gave him the stink eye but she noted Kristy just seemed afraid.

"What brings you out here—or do I even need to ask?"

Kristy laughed nervously. "Yeah, you got it. I want to be an actress. How about you?"

"Me too. Although life has interfered with my plans somewhat. I'm working as sort of a model just to make a few extra bucks."

"Ohh, a model! I'd like to do that too—you know, to get started. Who do you work with? How did you get started? Do you think they could use me?"

Heather laughed and held up her hands. "Whoa! Slow down!" She made a show of looking Kristy up and down. "Well, you certainly are pretty enough. Maybe if you lightened up your hair..." She paused. "Let me ask you some basics—the same things the agencies will ask. First of all, how old are you?"

"Eighteen."

Heather raised her eyebrows. "Really? 'Cause you don't look it." *Perfect,* she was thinking—*the younger-looking, the better.*

"Yeah, just turned eighteen three weeks ago."

"Wow. You look young—which is good in this town, let me tell you."

Kristy giggled. "Oh good."

"How tall are you?"

"Five-four."

"Hmm, might be a little short."

"You think?"

"Yeah, most of the top models are five-eight or so." Heather had no idea, really. It just sounded good to her. Besides, she didn't want the girl to develop any self-confidence. Now it was time to throw her a bone. "But your breasts, I must say, from a modeling perspective, well, they're perfect. Are they real?"

Kristy blushed and looked down at the sidewalk. "Uh, yeah."

Heather recognized that odd kind of embarrassment about her body. She guessed at once Kristy had been molested by an over-eager relative. Her father, stepfather or uncle. Maybe even a brother. She probably grew tired of fighting him off—or fucking him—and fled west as soon as she had graduated from high school. It was a sadly familiar story.

"So what made you pack up and come out all of a sudden?"

"Well, I've always wanted to, you know. Isn't that every girl's dream? Come out here and star in some movie or TV show? So after I graduated, I decided, 'now or never.' You know?"

Heather nodded. "Yeah. But it can be tough to break in here. I hope you're not expecting to be discovered overnight."

"Oh, uh, no. I guess not. I mean, I'll do what I have to do to work my way up."

"Are your parents backing you?" It was a key question and Heather kept an eye on Kristy's face when she asked it.

"Uh, no." She looked away, pain evident on her face.

Heather hid her smile. *Can I peg 'em or can I peg 'em?* she thought. "Oh. You plannin' on surprisin' them when you suddenly show up in a movie?"

"Yeah, something like that."

They reached the end of the block and Heather paused to let Kristy soak in the tawdry scene around them. The bus station was in the worst part of Hollywood—and there really weren't that many good parts. Back in the twenties, Hollywood probably seemed like paradise to most of those in the frozen Midwest, but over the years, it had attracted too many of the poor and wild-eyed dreamers. This led to a gradual decline in the populace as they began to feed on each other in order to survive. Too many today were humanity's cast-offs: Crazies, drunks, street preachers—and whores. Lots of whores.

"You don't have any support system out here? No relatives or friends you can call on?" This was important, for the ideal girl would be completely alone.

"No. Just me."

"That's pretty brave."

"Yeah, I'm beginning to realize that."

The light changed and Heather started across, walking quickly. "It's not much further."

They crossed and Kristy hurried to catch up. Heather was walking fast on purpose. She wanted the girl to develop a strong desire to stay with her so she wouldn't be left alone in this scary place. It helped bond them. They walked another block until they came to one of the sleaziest motels in town: The El Rancho, know universally in the neighborhood as the "El Rauncho."

"Here it is. Costs just forty-five bucks a night. Pretty cheap around here."

Kristy just stood and stared at it, her mouth ajar, taking in scene before her: The fading pink paint, the litter scattered across the parking lot, a huge, angry pimp arguing with a hooker in front of a graffiti-marred Coke machine, the room on the second floor with the broken window and the tattered remains of a crime scene tape still dangling from the doorknob. Heather waited for a long minute before she spoke up, putting false cheer in her voice.

"It's not so bad if you get a place on the second floor. Just be sure and lock your door. Maybe move some furniture in front of it."

"I-I-I can't...I can't stay here," Kristy said, shaking her head.

Worked every time. No innocent farm girl would be caught dead in a place like this. "Oh, well, if you can afford more, there's a place three blocks over that's much nicer."

"H-how much, do you think?"

"At the other place? Hmm. I think it's sixty-five a night. It's cleaner, and it's much quieter at night, so you can sleep."

Kristy began shaking her head and Heather saw the tears there. For a moment, she felt sorry for the poor, naïve girl. She remembered how she had felt, coming off the bus. She had fallen under the care of Maureen, another of Billy's bottom girls. But she was dead now from an overdose. It seemed so long ago Heather could hardly remember what her first day had been like.

"There must be something else," Kristy said. "A shelter? Something like that?"

There were two or three in Hollywood, Heather knew, aimed at teens just like Kristy. They were always crowded, but she could probably get some help from them. Or get advice to turn around and go home before it was too late.

"No, not really," she lied. "I mean, there's a shelter for abused women—I don't think they'd let you in, though. You aren't exactly abused, right?"

"Not yet."

"Well, come on, it won't be so bad." She started walking toward the El Rauncho and Kristy hurried to catch up.

"Wait, wait."

Heather stopped. "What?"

"I, uh..." She looked around, her face worried. "That nicer motel. You say it's sixty-five a night?"

Heather could see the calculations going on in her head and knew Kristy was figuring how long her money would last. She herself had arrived with just two hundred dollars and had stayed just two nights in a crappy motel before she succumbed to Maureen's siren call to share a room with her—and Billy. "Yeah, about. I'm not sure—I haven't stayed there in a long time. It might be a little more now."

Kristy bit her lip. "Well, okay, I guess."

Heather led her down a dirty street to the Aladdin Hotel, a step up from El Rauncho, but not by much. It was a two-story motel laid on two sides of a parking lot that faced a busy intersection. At least there were no broken windows or hookers, although the place hadn't been upgraded since the eighties.

"Oh, that's better," Kristy said, looking relieved.

"Come on." Heather led her across the street and waited while she checked in. The price had risen to seventy-three a night, including tax. She watched as Kristy pulled out a wad of bills with shaking hands and paid for one night.

"Thanks," Kristy said as they walked out. "I guess I'm all set."

"Sure," Heather said. "You gonna be all right?"

"I guess so."

"Tell ya what. I don't live too far away. I'll give you my cell phone number and you call if you need somethin'. Okay?"

"Oh, that would be great! You've been so nice."

"Hey, we girls gotta stick together, right? I mean, this town can be rough if you're not ready for it."

"I do feel a bit overwhelmed."

Heather jotted down her number and passed it over. Kristy seemed hesitant to let her go.

"Do you know of anyone who maybe needs a roommate?"

Heather recognized it at once as a desperate attempt to determine if Kristy might crash on her couch. She didn't rise to the bait—yet. It was too soon.

"No, but I can ask around. Okay, I'd better go. You sure you'll be all right?"

"Yeah, I guess."

Heather left, stopping once to wave at Kristy as the poor girl headed to her room. Give her two days, she thought. She'll be almost out of money and desperate for someone to help her.

Unless, of course, she wins a movie role first.

Heather laughed all the way back to her apartment.

CHAPTER TWO

Kristy sat on the bed and looked around. It was a motel room like a million others: bed, dresser, cheap TV, framed watercolor on the wall. It wasn't much, but it would do for now. She couldn't help but feel elated. She had made it! Hollywood! It had been terrifying, yes, but at least she'd found a decent place—and she'd already made a friend! Wouldn't it be great if she got a modeling job out of it?

Heather hadn't looked like the type to be a model. She was only an inch or two taller than Kristy was. Her blonde hair was clearly dyed and she seemed a bit cheap-looking with her heavy makeup on. But that was probably just Kristy's dated Midwestern values talking. It was certainly different in Hollywood! There were people everywhere who looked a lot like Heather: Tanned, artificial and savvy. She wished she was savvy—she could use that confidence.

She stood and went to the mirror and looked at herself. She turned this way and that, thrusting out her breasts and smiling. Everyone loved her tits, she thought. Her mood instantly darkened. Especially her father. The drunken asshole. Fathers aren't supposed to touch daughters like that.

She focused on her face and pulled her hair back out of the way. *Maybe Heather was right—I would look better as a full-on blonde. I'd have to do something with those eyebrows.*

All that was for later, she decided. First things first. She sat on the bed and pulled out her wallet. Dumping all her cash onto the bed, she counted it out. Twenty, forty, sixty, eighty, one hundred. Twenty, forty, sixty. She had a ten and two fives left. One hundred eighty total. And that was after she had paid for the room.

God, the money had gone so fast! She had swiped more than four hundred dollars from her father before she fled. She would've loved to have seen his face when he discovered his stash was gone! With the bus tickets and meals and now a motel room, she calculated she had just two days to find a job. Or else.

She shivered when she thought about being alone on the streets.

Kristy checked her watch. Little after two. Might as well do some research now. She found the phone book and looked up Modeling Agencies and Actors Agencies and began making calls.

"Hello? My name is Kristy Carnes and I'm an actress looking for work..."

She usually got no further than the secretary. Some were downright rude. Others simply said, "We're not taking any representations at this time" and hung up. She didn't give up. There was nothing else for her to do.

Only one woman was nice. She asked her, "Whatcha been in, honey?"

"Uh, nothing yet. I'm hoping to break in—"

The woman laughed. "Wouldn't we all! You have a snowball's chance in hell, unless you know somebody. You got a friend, a relative in the business?"

"Uh, no."

"Too bad. Have you checked Variety?"

Kristy had heard of it but had never seen one. "You mean, the magazine?"

"No, honey, it's a newspaper. It's only the bible of actors. If you don't know Variety, you're wasting everyone's time." She hung up.

Shit, Kristy thought. She got up at once and went out. She found a newsstand two blocks away and bought a Variety, Hollywood Reporter and a SAG magazine. The newsstand clerk gave her a knowing wink when he handed them over.

"Good luck, sweetie."

"Uh, thanks."

She took her purchases back to the motel and locked herself inside. Kristy spent the rest of the afternoon and early evening reading. In the back of the Reporter, she found an ad for "open auditions" the following day. They were casting unknowns for a new, independent movie. Maybe that would be her chance! She wrote down the address and went to sleep dreaming of stardom.

She arrived early at the auditions to find two hundred people already in line. Her heart sank. She stood at the back and noticed how much better everyone looked than she did. They had on expensive clothes, smooth makeup and perfect hair. Even the men displayed that plastic Hollywood appearance. Kristy felt out of place.

She also noticed nearly everyone had a portfolio or manila envelope. References, she thought with a panic. They've brought references. *All I have is my face.* She hoped it would be enough.

Kristy waited three hours in the hot sun until she made her way to the door. Once inside, she had to wait another thirty minutes to work her way to the table, where two men and a woman sat in a large room.

"Next!"

Taking a deep breath, she strode up to them and said, "Hi, I'm Kristy Carnes." She gave them her most dazzling smile.

A bearded young man eyed her up and down. "Whatcha been in?" he asked abruptly.

"Uh, some high school plays. I'm new—"

He looked pained. "Gimme your resume and book," he demanded in a bored tone, his hand held out, palm up.

Her heart stopped. "Uh, I don't have one right now." She wasn't even sure what a book was.

His face darkened. "Fuck! How're we supposed to know who you are if you don't have a resume? Jesus!" He looked past her. "Next!"

The man to his right muttered, "Fuckin' amateurs." Only the woman, a brunette wearing a baseball cap with a pigtail sticking out the back, looked at her with some sympathy.

Tears began to fill Kristy's eyes. "I didn't know...I can get one." She didn't know what she'd put in it—two high school productions? Still, she should've known! She saw everyone else with something!

"Lady, step aside, we gotta lotta people waiting."

Ears burning, Kristy moved back and stumbled for the door. Her head was roaring with embarrassment and she couldn't bear to feel their disdainful eyes on her. She paused to catch her breath and felt a hand on her arm. She turned to see the pigtailed woman from the table.

"Hey, it's all right. You'll be all right," she said.

"I'm so sorry! I didn't know what to bring!"

"So you're new here in town?"

Kristy nodded.

"Okay, just so you know the next time you come to one of these. You need a resume containing all your acting experience. Anything you've done." She looked around and added in a whisper, "And a lot of people embellish." She winked.

"Thank you, you're so kind."

"You also should have a book. You know, shots of your face and of recent roles, if you have any. Or in different poses."

"Oh!" That sounded expensive.

The woman patted her arm again. "You have a very pretty face. You might do well here."

"Thank you!" She didn't want this moment to end. "Uh, what's your name?"

"Sally. Sally Lindstrom."

"Thank you so much for being kind. I'll never forget this."

Sally smiled and tipped her head. "You're welcome. Hope to see you at another of these someday."

"Oh, you will!"

Feeling much better, she strode past the line of hopefuls and left the building. She stopped by a grocery store to buy a banana for lunch and she asked the clerk where the library was. Eating the banana on the way, Kristy imagined what "roles" she might be able to fake. Because she was just eighteen, it would be hard to make up too much or a casting director would know she was lying. Perhaps she could say she won a junior beauty pageant...and starred in a local TV commercial for a car dealership...Yes, that would work.

By the time she reached the library, Kristy had a decent resume made up. She found an unused computer and tried to sign on. "Library Card Number" the computer demanded. The help desk informed her she had to sign up and give a permanent address before she could use the computers.

"But I don't have a permanent address yet!" she told the librarian.

"I'm sorry, but it's policy. Otherwise, you might check out a book and never return it."

"I don't want to check out a book, I just want to use the computer!"

The librarian studied her. "Well, if that's all you want to do, I suppose I could sign you in. But I can only give you twenty minutes."

"Thank you!" Maybe this town wasn't so heartless after all, she thought. Already, she'd met two decent human beings.

Working feverishly, Kristy managed to make up a quick resume and printed out two copies in thirty-five minutes— the librarian had given her extra time when she saw what the young woman was working on. The finished product wasn't much and the paper looked cheap, but it would do for a start. She could always go to a print shop and have it done on professional heavyweight bond. Looking it over, she tried to imagine a casting director studying it.

She had played Queen Guenevere in "A Connecticut Yankee in King Author's Court" and one of the orphans in "Oliver Twist." Those had been real high school roles. She added the fake junior pageant and the car commercial and felt she had a decent, if padded, resume. She had used the motel's phone number as hers and wished she had money enough to obtain a cell phone. She'd have to do that with her first earnings, she decided.

Kristy returned to her motel and paid for another day, watching another seventy-three dollars disappear from her stash. A little over one hundred dollars left. She had one more day to find a job. That was her problem, she realized. Instead of trying for the big score, she should be looking for a waitressing job or something like that.

She bought a Los Angeles Times outside the office and returned to her room. Perusing the want ads, Kristy selected about five possibilities. She realized her resume was all wrong, but they probably wouldn't ask for it anyway. Not for a minimum wage job.

Checking her watch, she felt she had wasted much of her day standing in line. That had been foolish, although she had learned some valuable information. Kristy grabbed the want ads and one copy of her resume and headed out. Riding buses back and forth to job sites was exhausting. She managed to cover just three possibilities before she grew discouraged and headed home. No one had offered a job outright. The last place—an upscale restaurant—had said they might call in "in a few days."

Kristy hadn't the nerve to tell them that if they didn't call by tomorrow, she'd be out on the street. She feared it would've sounded too desperate.

In talking to managers, she quickly realized that the jobs she sought paid minimum wage or slightly better. That meant, after taxes, she'd have to work ten hours a day or get amazing tips just to be able to afford her motel room! It was impossible. No, a regular job would only prevent her from achieving her dream and yet she had to have *some* money coming in.

Kristy sat in her room and cried, despairing what to do. She could pay for just one more night and then what? Go to a shelter? Go home? Heck, she couldn't even afford to do that!

She remembered the young woman she had met, Heather. She worked for a modeling agency, she had said. Maybe she could help her. With shaking fingers, she dialed the phone.

CHAPTER THREE

Oh, hi, Kristy! How's it going?" Heather smiled when she got the call. She had planned to stop by and visit Kristy tomorrow, to see how she was doing. Hearing her voice on the phone, she could tell at once the farm girl was already panicking.

"Hi, Heather! It's, uh, going okay. I was, uh, wondering if you asked at the modeling agency if they needed someone like me?"

"Yeah, I did. They said they'd like to see your book."

"Oh. My book, yeah. Um…"

"Yeah, you know, your photos of past work. Could be from your plays and stuff or just face shots."

"I don't have anything like that yet."

"Oh, too bad. They won't look at anyone without a book." Heather heard a suppressed sob. "What's wrong?"

"I'm, I'm running out of money! And I haven't found a job that'll pay me enough to live!" Heather heard Kristy ramble on about her disastrous effort at the casting call and realized this girl was primed and ready! Time to throw her a lifeline.

"Why don't I come out and see you? I have to be in the area today anyway. Maybe we could come up with something."

"Oh, would you!? That would be great!"

Heather set up a time and hung up. She turned to see Billy studying her, his dark eyes glittering. "She's nearly ready."

He smiled. "Good. She's that cute one you told me about, right? From Bumfuck, Iowa or someplace?"

"Right. Kristy Carnes. Already sounds like a porn star."

He laughed. "Good. Good job, sweetie." He came over and gave her a hug and squeezed her bottom. Heather shivered in his masculine grip. Billy was a tall, strong man and he always knew how to excite her. "If she's ready, bring her by around five—I'll be sure and be here."

"Sure," she said, thinking about how Billy would turn on the charm. The poor girl didn't stand a chance with the handsome pimp.

Heather knocked on Kristy's door and the girl opened it at once. "Oh, Heather!" She gave the whore a quick hug. "I'm so glad to see you!"

"Hi, Kristy. Nice place you got here," she said, coming inside. "I woulda killed for a place like this when I first got into town!"

"But it's so expensive! I was hoping to find a cheaper place. At least until I get a good job."

Heather could see the fright in the girl's eyes. She had no idea what to do next. She almost felt sorry for her. But then, Kristy was sitting on a gold mine, if she got desperate enough to use it.

Kristy brought her up to date on her adventures and admitted she had only enough cash for one more night at the motel. Heather pretended to be shocked.

"Shit, girl, you came out here with just a couple hundred?"

"It was all I could get!"

"I don't know. Maybe you shoulda stayed at that other motel—you could've lasted another day or two."

"That won't help me now! I gotta find something quick! Can you think of something?"

"Hmm," Heather pretended to mull it over. She wasn't sure Kristy was desperate enough yet. "Depends on what you're willing to do to survive."

Kristy didn't pick up on the innuendo. "Oh, I'd flip burgers, I'd wait tables—just about anything!"

Heather sneered. "Those jobs pay shit. I'm talking about modeling jobs that might involve a little skin. You don't need a book for those."

Kristy's mouth made a comical 'O'. She didn't speak for a moment. When her voice returned, she said, "Oh, no, I couldn't do that. I came out to be an actress, not a porn star!"

Heather shrugged. "Suit yourself. Maybe you could wire home and ask for some cash to tide you over."

"No, no I can't do that, either. They don't know where I've gone."

"Really? Hell, I can relate to that! I left town so fast, I was in Hollywood before my folks even knew I was missing."

Kristy nodded. "Yeah. I don't ever want to see them again."

"Must've been tough." She didn't pry for there was no need to. Substitute her own experience and that's probably what Kristy had gone through. She felt a kinship to the girl that she realized she could use. Time for a bit of a confession. "I left home because my stepdad was getting frisky, if you know what I mean."

Kristy's eyes grew wide. "Yes!" She didn't say anything further, but Heather could read it in her face. Poor girl. She wondered if it was a stepdad, uncle, brother or father. It was almost always a relative. Fucking men.

"It was almost enough to make me give up on men," Heather said.

Kristy nodded. She immediately changed the subject. "Um, I was wondering…" Heather waited—she knew what was coming. "Do you know of any place I could crash? Like on someone's couch? Just for a few days," she added hurriedly.

She was broadly hinting and it was time for Heather to make her understand the situation. "Well, I don't live alone or I'd invite you to stay with me."

"Oh! I'm sorry, I didn't mean…"

"No, it's all right. I like you, kid. You remind me of me a few years ago. But I live with Billy, he runs the modeling agency, you see. It's actually his apartment."

"Oh! You're so lucky!"

"No, it's not like that. I mean, we used to be romantic at one time, but not anymore. Now we're just roommates for a while." A very short while, she knew. If she fell out of Billy's favor, she'd wind up back in the crib with the other girls and he'd appoint a new bottom girl. It happened all the time. She was determined to stay in his swanky apartment as long as she could, even if it meant throwing young girls like Kristy to the wolves. "He wouldn't want me to bring stray girls home unless they're modeling for him."

"Well, I'd love to model…" She caught Heather's look. "Oh, you mean, that kind of modeling."

"Yeah. I'm sorry."

"No, I'm sorry, I didn't mean…I just mean, if you know anybody else, that's all."

"Oh, I'm sorry! I promised to ask around, didn't I?" She watched as Kristy's face fell. "I'm so sorry! I promise, I'll do that today."

"That would be great!"

"Okay. Well, I'd better go. I'm sure you've got lots of jobs to check out and stuff."

"Yeah," Kristy said with false enthusiasm. "Sure."

She left the poor farm girl standing in the doorway, looking like a puppy that had just been kicked. But Heather could tell that Kristy wasn't quite desperate enough. Her quick rejection of the modeling job she'd held out had proved that. No, she needed to marinate another day or two. Wait until she was completely broke and tossed out onto the street with her suitcase. Then she might consider alternatives—nude modeling or hooking. Billy knew how to turn on the charm and within a month, Kristy would become just another whore in his stable.

"You call me and keep me posted, all right? Don't get yourself into trouble now."

"I won't."

Yeah, leave that to me, she thought.

Heather returned to the apartment. Billy was waiting. "Well?" he asked.

"She's not quite ready. I hinted about modeling nude and she rejected it flat out. Didn't even want to know how much it paid."

Billy shrugged. "Okay. Keep me posted." He checked his watch. "Meanwhile, why don't you go out and earn some money, hmm?"

Her shoulders sagged. "Aw, Billy, I thought I'd get a little break from—" She stopped when she saw Billy's darkening expression. "Yeah, okay." She knew better than to push it too far. She went to her room and put on one of her "fuck me" outfits—a stretchy pink mini-dress that form-fit her body, coming to just below the vee of her legs. No need for a bra— her tits were small and firm. She slipped on a pair of thong panties and stuck her feet into lavender three-inch heels and she was ready.

She waved goodbye and headed down to see Ronald, Billy's driver and enforcer. He lived on the first floor. He opened the door to her knock and winked at her, his bald head gleaming in the lights. "Hey, Heather, you're lookin' good." Ronald was a broad-shouldered African-American with an easy disposition that hid a mean mother-fucker underneath. Cross him once and you'd never want to do it again. Heather had personally seen him beat a john nearly to death with his fists, after the john had dared to injure one of Billy's whores. She'd also been on the receiving end of one of his "whore beat-downs" when she failed to make her quota for the evening. It was the last time she had come up short. He had been careful to beat her in such a way that she ached all over the next day, but had few visible bruises, so she wouldn't miss any work.

Ronald had the disposition to be a decent pimp himself, but lacked the smarts. So he hung around Billy, driving the girls and acting tough, happy in his more limited role. She knew Billy paid him well—why would he ever want to aspire to more?

"Come on, sweetheart, let's see it."

Sighing, she raised up her skirt to show him her thong right there in the hallway. He loved sexy underwear—or pussies. All the girls had to flash him before he'd drive them. Billy didn't care as long as he didn't waste time fucking them.

"Pretty. Okay, let's go."

She followed him to the garage and slid into the passenger seat of the black Escalade. Ronald drove her down to her "corner"—a prime spot near Melrose and La Brea. She stepped down from the SUV and looked around. Ronald waved and drove off. He'd make the rounds and check back with her regularly. She also kept in touch by phone—at the first sign of trouble, he'd show up in minutes to beat up an abusive john or smooth-talk the cops.

Heather checked her watch. It was just six—a bit too late for the commuters and too early for the night trade. She began walking up and down the block, smiling at everyone who honked at her.

Fortunately, a regular pulled up, getting Heather into the mood for work when she recognized him. Joe was a nice Jewish guy, married to an uptight woman who would never give him a blowjob if her life depended on it. Ha! If only wives would realize that what a man can't get at home, he can always find somewhere else. She leaned into the passenger side window.

"Hi, Joe!"

"Hi, Heather. I need you—I'm all backed up. Hop in!"

"Sure." She climbed in and he drove to their special spot, behind a Long's Drug Store a block away. He parked and eased the seat back. She unzipped him and fished out his hard cock.

"Ooooh, I remember you," she cooed. She enveloped it at once, hearing a satisfied sigh from Joe. He'd been right—he was primed and ready for this. She felt his hips start to jerk within minutes and tickled his balls just the way he liked and he shot into her mouth. Heather swallowed quickly and pulled back.

"Boy, you were horny, honey!"

"Thanks, you're a dear. My fuckin' wife, you know..."

Heather laughed. "Sure, baby. Sure."

Joe pulled out his wallet and peeled of three fifties and handed them over. "Here ya go. Best mouth in Hollywood."

"Thanks, Joe." She slipped the money into her bra as Joe drove her back. She gave him a wave and got out. As she drove off, she felt better. Her self-pity was gone—now she could concentrate on making a living.

CHAPTER FOUR

K risty went out the next morning to renew her search for a job—she was determined to take anything as long as it was steady. She found an opening at a Burger King and grabbed it, despite the pay: Just seven-fifty an hour. If she worked eight hours a day, she'd only clear fifty dollars, after taxes. She had to find a new place to live!

Rusty, the manager, seemed more interested in her as a potential girlfriend than a worker. He was an overweight, pimply-faced man in his early twenties with wildly uncombed brown hair. He said she could start the next day, "working side by side with me until you learned the ropes."

Kristy hid her disgust and thanked him. "Uh..." she began, trying to find the most delicate way to ask the next question. "Rusty, can you tell me how often we get paid?"

"Every two weeks. But it takes a week to process everything, so everyone's a week behind. So you'll get your first check in three weeks."

She stared at him. "Three weeks?"

"Yeah. Is that a problem?"

"Uh." She tried to think of how she might manage. "Can I get an advance, just to tide me over?"

"Heck no! Otherwise, we'd have a lot of people get the advance and take off."

Kristy nodded, trying to figure out how she could survive three weeks. Nothing made sense. Unless she was willing to sleep in a car or someone's couch...

She thought of Heather again and wondered if her only friend in town had talked to any of her friends. Maybe there was a way around this.

"Well?" Rusty was studying her. "You want the job or not?"

She made a quick decision. A dead-end job that doesn't pay enough to live or take a chance that Heather has found something that will give her a few extra days to land a modeling or acting job. "Sorry, Rusty. I can't afford to work here." She got up and headed for the door, leaving Rusty standing there speechless for a moment. As she reached the front door, Kristy heard his voice ringing in her ears: "What? You're too good for us?"

Got that right, she thought.

By the time she returned to the motel, despair had set in. She had been foolish to turn it down, despite her distaste for both the job and the manager. Where else was she going to find a good job while she went on auditions? Everything she tried seemed hopeless. She was heading to her room when she heard her name being called. She turned to see Amir, the manager, waving to her. Her heart sank. She trudged over to him.

"Hello, Ms. Carnes," he said. "I want to know if you stay another night?" He bobbed his head and smiled.

"Uh, I don't know, maybe," she said. Her heart pounded.

"Good! We're glad to have you. Come on in and we take care of it, okay?"

"Oh, can't I pay you later?" *Like day after tomorrow?* she was thinking.

"No, no. Pay in advance or move out by noon. That's how we run things here." His head kept bobbing and it made Kristy want to reach out and make it stop.

"You can't let me stay here for a couple of days if I promise to pay you for sure by Friday?"

"No, no. Must pay. In advance. Everybody pays."

She nodded and followed him like a condemned woman heading for the gallows. She stalled as long as she could in front of the counter, counting and recounting her money down inside her purse where Amir couldn't see.

She had just fifty-seven dollars left. Not enough to pay for another night.

"Um, I'm a little short. Would you take fifty for the room?"

Amir frowned. "No no! I no make acceptions." He used the wrong word, but Kristy knew what he meant.

"It's just temporary! I'm looking for jobs every day. I almost got one today!"

He kept shaking his head. "You no pay, out by noon. That is rules."

Kristy felt tears come to her eyes. She couldn't get a break from this hard-headed man! A wicked thought came to her. "How...How 'bout if I show you my breasts? Would you take fifty for the room then?"

He stopped shaking his head and tipped it to one side. "I don't know. Let me see first."

"You'll take fifty for the room?" she insisted.

"Let me see what is worth so much," he said stubbornly.

Sighing, Kristy pulled up her shirt, taking her bra with it, giving Amir a quick glance at her bare breasts before yanking it back down again.

"There! Okay?"

He shook his head. "Very nice, but not worth money. You pay seventy-three or get out."

Kristy was incredulous. "What!? I showed you! You promised!"

"I did not. I say, I want to see if they worth it. They not."

Humiliated and embarrassed, Kristy fled toward her room, feeling like a fool.

"I'll find something," she whispered. "I'll find something."

She thought about returning to Burger King and getting that job after all. She could grovel a bit and she was sure Rusty would relent. But even as she thought about it, she knew that was a dead-end solution. She needed a job that paid a decent wage.

Hmm. Heather had said she could get a job in modeling if she was willing to show some skin. How much skin and how much money? Kristy went to the phone and dialed Heather's number.

Heather came awake groggily when her cell phone rang. She focused a bleary eye on the clock. Eleven-fifteen. God. Who was calling at this ungodly hour? She hadn't gotten in until after three a.m. She snatched the phone from the nightstand.

"'Lo?"

"Heather?"

She came awake at once when she realized it was Kristy. She had reached that panic point, Heather could tell. She tried to inject some false cheer into her voice.

"Oh, hi, Kristy! What's up! Did you find a job?"

"No! Well, yes. But I had to turn it down! It doesn't pay enough to let me live!" Heather listened as Kristy babbled on about her morning.

"Those jobs are dead-end anyway," she commiserated when Kristy had finished. "They never want to let you out to audition and they're always hassling you for one thing or another. You were smart to walk away."

"But I've got nowhere to go and my money's gone!" She wailed over the phone.

Heather waited, smiling. Poor girl.

"Uh, I wanted to ask you if you asked around and found someone willing to put me up for a couple days? You know, like someone who maybe was in my position a while back who'd like to help a girl out?"

"I've only had time to ask one girl and she couldn't," Heather lied. She had asked no one, of course. "But I'll ask a few more by next week. Maybe you could call me again on Tuesday?"

"I'll be out on the street by then!"

"I'm sorry. Hollywood is a tough town, that's for sure."

There came a pause that lengthened until Heather thought they might've gotten disconnected.

"Hello?"

"No, I'm here. I was just thinking."

Here it comes, she thought.

"What...uh, what does that modeling job pay? The one you mentioned?"

"Oh, I don't know if you want to do that. It's nude or semi-nude stuff. You know. I mean, it's artfully done, but you didn't sound like that was for you."

"Well, how much does it pay?"

"I think it's three hundred a sitting."

"Three hundred? Like, cash?"

"Yeah."

"Wow. That sounds...Did you do that?"

"I did. For a while anyway. It's only a temporary gig. They're always looking for fresh faces."

"You think they'd like me?"

"Oh, sure! I mean, if you wanted to do it. They'd love your face." Not to mention your tits and your pussy, Heather thought.

"I, uh...I think I might want to do it. Can you help me set it up?"

"Sure. I have ask Billy—he's in charge of all that. He'll want to see you, of course. Why don't I call you back around two?"

"Oh! That'll be too late! I have to leave my motel pretty soon."

"Well, wait outside and I'll come by at two, okay?"

"Thank you, Heather! You're a life-saver!"

Heather hung up the phone, shook her head in disbelief at how easy it was, rolled over and went back to sleep.

An hour and a half later, she roused herself up, slipped on her robe and went to find Billy. He was up drinking coffee and reading the paper in his boxer shorts. He smiled when he spotted Heather.

"Hey, dollface. Be a dear and give me a quickie, willya?" He pushed himself away from the table and spread his legs. His semi-hard cock tented his shorts.

"Wait—I gotta call from that girl. Kristy? You remember?"

He paused. "Oh yeah, the farm girl. What's up? Is she ready for me?"

"Yes. She just called a while ago. She's out of money and said she might like to model nude. She seemed a bit freaked out by it, but I think she'll go through with it."

"What about her living arrangements?"

"She needs a place bad. She's already hinted that I put her up on the couch."

Billy nodded. "Good." He took another sip of coffee. "Okay, get busy. You call her later and bring her over. I want to get a good look at my new whore."

Her mouth was still a bit sore from last night—as was her pussy!—and she hadn't had any coffee yet, but she knew better than to keep Billy waiting. Heather bent down and eased his cock out of his shorts and began to fellate him. He leaned back against the chair and sighed contentedly.

"Oh yeah, baby, that's it," he said, giving her a playful slap on the face. She grimaced and kept going. Billy liked to slap his bitches as he had sex with them. It was just his thing. She endured several more slaps before she felt his balls start to boil and really began to slide her mouth up and down his hard shaft. With a sudden cry, he ejaculated down her throat and she swallowed at once.

"Good girl. You're my favorite whore, you know that?"

She smiled. "Can I have some coffee now?"

"Sure babe. Pour me another cup."

At two-fifteen, Heather found Kristy sitting outside the motel with her small valise in tow. She looked frightened and bedraggled. She brightened at once when she spotted Heather.

"Oh, thanks! I thought you weren't coming!" She jumped into the passenger seat.

"Got hung up a bit," she said. Actually, she had planned to be a few minutes late to help increase Kristy's anxiety and to form a stronger bond between the two of them. She was her savior now—Kristy would listen to her advice. Billy would take care of the rest.

"Did you talk to your friend? Billy?"

"Yeah. He wants to meet you."

"Oh, good." She sat back, the valise in her lap, her knees jerking nervously.

"Hey, relax. You seem tense."

"I am! I'm so nervous! What if he doesn't like me?"

Heather suppressed a smile. "Oh, I think he'll like you. You're right up his alley." *Cute, dumb and sexy,* she thought.

"You really think so?"

"Oh, yes. I know Billy loves you wholesome farm girl types."

"I didn't grow up on a farm."

"No matter. You still have the look."

They arrived at the apartment building and Heather escorted Kristy up the elevator. "Now just be yourself," she told the nervous girl before she unlocked the door to the apartment.

* * *

Kristy walked in and was stunned by the beauty of the place. It was like a showroom apartment. The décor was modern and sleek and looked like something from a Town and Country layout. The theme was black and white and it clearly had been professionally done. The white couch was huge and Kristy could picture herself sleeping on it. She pushed the thought out of her mind. The full-length French doors opened out onto a balcony that overlooked the city. She walked around, oohing and ahhing over the place.

"Nice, huh?"

"Wow, it's great!"

"Wait here, I'll get Billy." Heather disappeared down the hall.

Kristy walked about, afraid to touch anything. A shelf contained what appeared to be antique vases and plates. On the walls were artworks by some avant-garde painters that she thought might be worth a fortune. She made her way to the French door and gazed out at the panoramic view.

"Hello," she heard a voice behind her and whirled about to see a tall, athletic man in his mid-thirties standing there, dressed in jeans and a black T-shirt. Heather was nowhere to be seen.

"H-Hello," she said, coming toward him, her hand outstretched. "I'm Kristy."

"I'm Billy."

Her first impression of Billy was one of strength. His muscles bulged underneath his T-shirt and his stomach was flat. His face seemed kindly, but it had an undercurrent of danger to it. She couldn't help but be impressed. No wonder Heather had fallen for him! She wondered if he had a girlfriend. Probably did. This guy could have any girl he wanted!

He shook her hand, his eyes coolly appraising her. She felt a flush of embarrassment creep up her neck and tried to fake nonchalance.

"Heather told me you'd like to model, but she didn't tell me how beautiful you were."

Her blush deepened. "Th-thank you."

"So, you just got into town?"

"Yes, a few days ago. From Indiana. Trying to become an actress." She felt she was babbling.

Billy nodded. "I can see the look. You have it."

Kristy wasn't sure what he meant, but she was enormously flattered nonetheless. "Thank you."

"Turn around."

She pirouetted, trying not to feel foolish. She could feel his eyes devouring her.

"Very nice," he said. "Now, let me see the rest."

Kristy paused, confused. "The...rest?" She knew what he meant, of course, but fear still gripped her.

He waggled his fingers. "Yes. Take off your clothes." He seemed impatient.

Her mouth came open and she fought for breath. "Uh....
Uh..."

His expression softened at once. "Oh, I'm sorry. Didn't
Heather explain? I'm looking for nude and semi-nude
models."

"Y-yes, she said that. It...It's just sudden, you know."

"My apologies. Would you feel more comfortable if
Heather was in the room? I can call her."

Kristy realized this was her big chance. *Don't blow it!
Stop being a baby!* "Yes, that would make me feel more, uh,
comfortable."

He strode to the hall and called, "Heather?"

She came out and joined them. "Everything okay?" she
asked Kristy.

"Yes," Billy answered for her. "But she's shy."

"Ohh," Heather nodded knowingly. "I see. Mind if I talk
to her?"

"No, not at all."

She came forward and grabbed Kristy's arm and escorted
her out onto the balcony, carefully closing the door behind
them.

"What's wrong? You want to back out?"

"I...I don't know. I-I was just startled by his cavalier
attitude, I guess."

"Honey, I went to some trouble to set this up. I talked you
up to Billy and made it sound like if he didn't snap you up,
someone else would. If you backed out now, I'll look bad, you
understand?"

"Oh! I'm sorry! I didn't mean..."

"It's okay. I know it's happening quickly. But that's how it
is here. You've got to grab whatever opportunities come your
way or go home. You want to go home?"

"No!" She didn't have the money for it anyway.

"Good. Now if you'll feel more comfortable, I'll stay in the room. But don't be a baby or he'll send you away and you'll miss out on this chance."

"I'm sorry! I'm okay now."

"Good. You want me to stay?"

Kristy thought about that and decided against it. She would be embarrassed enough as it was, being naked in front of this handsome stranger, let alone her new friend. "No, that's okay. You can go back to what you were doing."

"All right. Come on."

She followed Heather inside, her heart pounding.

"She'll be okay now," Heather told Billy. "I'm going to go back to my room."

"You sure?" Billy was looking at Kristy.

"Y-yes," she said.

Heather left and Billy stood in front of her. "I know this is nerve-wracking, but it's got to be done. I had a girl here last month, for example. She was beautiful! Flawless skin. But when she took off her blouse, she had a dragon tattoo that looked like it had been done with crayons! It was horrible."

"I see."

"Let's start slow, okay? Take off your blouse first. That's all."

Kristy unbuttoned her blouse and pulled the sides apart. Her heart beat so loudly, she was sure he could hear it. She shrugged the garment off her shoulders and laid it over a nearby chair. She stood before this man in her bra, heat spreading up from her chest to her cheeks.

"Good. Now was that so hard?"

It had been hard, but she shook her head.

"You have beautiful skin. No tattoos!"

Kristy smiled and felt marginally better.

"I'll give you the choice now. Skirt or bra."

She licked her lips and thought about it. Her fingers went to her side and she unclasped her skirt and let it fall to the carpet. She stepped out of it and bent down to pick it up and placed it on the chair. There seemed to be a buzzing in her head and she fought to keep from running from the room.

"You are beautiful. You really are." He walked around her, taking in her proportions. She jerked when she felt his hand gently touch the curve of her ass.

"Sorry, didn't mean to startle you. I was just checking the shape here."

"Uh huh."

He came back around to the front. "Are we ready for the next step?"

Kristy bit her lip. "Do you have to see everything?"

He nodded. "I can't promise a woman I can use her until I see what I'm getting. You can understand that, can't you?"

"W-what kind of pictures are we talking about? You said something about semi-nude?"

He nodded. "Yes, if you wish to do semi-nude, I know people who do that. But the pay is less."

That got her attention. "How much less?"

"Semi-nude shots are easy to come by. Now, you're a very pretty girl, so you might do okay, but I'd have to guess, you might get a hundred, maybe one-fifty, for a sitting."

One-fifty didn't sound bad. It would give her two more days at the hotel.

"Yeah, I'd like to do that."

Billy nodded. "Okay. Then we're done here. You can put on your clothes."

With great relief, she started to dress.

"I can call around, see who's shooting. I'll have Heather call you in a couple days." He headed for the hall.

Kristy froze. "Uh...sir..."

He turned. "Yes?"

"I thought...I thought you did shots like that. I mean, your business."

"Yes, we do on occasion, but mostly we do nude shots. The market for them is better. That's why I was going to have to ask around."

"You, er, don't know of anything today? Or tomorrow?"

"Why, what's the rush?"

"I, uh, don't have any place to live." She felt hot tears come to her eyes and she fought them, not wanting to appear weak in front of this man.

Billy frowned. "How could you not have a place to live? I thought you came to Hollywood to be a star?"

"I did! I want to be. I...I just ran out of money."

"So soon?" He seemed incredulous. "Things don't happen overnight here, honey."

"I know, it's just...I couldn't get any more money together before I left." She felt like crying again.

He nodded slowly. "That's tough. I know this can be an expensive town. Maybe you could find a place with friends?"

"Heather is my only friend, so far."

He seemed surprised. He called down the hall. "Heather!"

The blonde reappeared. "Yes?"

"Did you try to find Kristy a place to stay?"

"Yes, I did. I asked a few of the girls I know. But no one wanted to share a space with someone they didn't know. You know how it is. But I'm still asking around."

Kristy got up her nerve and said, "Do you think, uh, maybe I could stay here a day or two? Just on your couch?"

Billy's head swiveled around. He frowned. He turned back to Heather. "Did you put her up to this?" His voice had an edge that frightened Kristy.

"No. No I didn't. I told her the deal here, that you owned the place."

He studied her for a moment. Kristy felt embarrassed for asking. She piped up, "It was my idea, uh, sir. I'm sorry. I thought if I was working for you and all..."

"But you aren't, are you? Why would I put you up in my very expensive place if you're going to do a photo shoot with one of my competitors?"

"Are...they competitors?" She was confused. Didn't he say they only did semi-nude shots?

"Yes, all photographers are competitors in this town. Because this town is built on relationships. Say you went to another photographer and through that guy you nabbed a commercial. And during that commercial shoot, someone asks you to recommend a photographer for another job. Now who are you gonna recommend—me or that other photographer?"

Kristy thought it was a rhetorical question, so she said nothing.

"Come on, Billy, the girl just needs a break. Couldn't you let her stay here for just the night? It's already getting late."

He frowned and said nothing.

Kristy took the hint. "I'm sorry," she said, gathering up her things. "I'll just go—I didn't mean to cause trouble."

She got to the door with her small suitcase, not knowing where she might go from here. Tears clouded her vision.

"Wait," she heard behind her. She turned expectantly.

"I guess I have been kind of a jerk," Billy said, his voice friendly again. "Tell you what—you can stay here tonight. Aw, heck, I'll let you stay a couple days—but you gotta agree to pay me something. I'm not running a charity for homeless girls."

"Oh, sure, yes, that's the least I can do!" she gushed, not having any idea how she might do that.

"What were you paying at that motel?"

"Uh, seventy-three a night."

He chuckled. "This place costs me more'n two hundred a night to rent! But I'll give you a break, okay? I'll only charge you fifty bucks a night—that's far less than what you paid at that fleabag motel."

Kristy had no idea how she would pay him, but she jumped at the offer. "That would be great! Oh, thanks, sir!"

"Call me Billy. Everybody does."

"Okay Billy. Thanks."

"And you'll remember me when you're famous and you'll throw me some jobs, right?"

"You bet!"

"Okay. But try to stay outta the way, okay?"

"I promise!" She returned to the living room and eyed her new bed. She wasn't sure how it all would work, but she was thrilled for this chance. But she thought she should explain her situation to Billy so there wouldn't be any misunderstandings.

"Uh, Billy...I can't pay you right away..."

He waved a hand. "I know you're struggling. You get a decent gig in the next two or three days and I'll let you slide. But then you gotta pay me and move out, understood?"

"Oh, yes, sir! Thank you so much!"

"Yeah, okay."

Heather came forward and threw her arms around Kristy. "I'm glad you're staying here a few days. I hope you land something soon!"

"I will go out every day! I'll get something!"

"Come on, you can store your bag in my room until it's time for bed."

Kristy gave Billy a big smile as she followed Heather down the hall, past the closed door to Billy's suite, to her room. "Room," as it turned out, was really not much more than a closet. She guessed it had meant to be a den that had been converted. Heather had a twin bed up against one wall under a small window and a tiny dresser that the door banged into when she opened it. Not much else would fit. But to Kristy, it was heaven.

"As you can see, it's kinda small," Heather said.

"No, it's cute!" She wished she had a room in a fancy pad like this. She wondered what Heather paid for it, but was afraid to ask directly.

"So you and Billy were together and then you broke up, but he still lets you rent the room? That's cool," she said, fishing for information.

Heather nodded. "Sorta. We only dated for a little while. And I sometimes have to take turns renting this room with some other girls."

"Oh." Kristy didn't understand and her face showed it.

"I mean, he has models coming in and out. Sometimes, I have to go bunk with some other girls in another place he rents. Kinda dorm-style."

Kristy wondered at once if there would be room for her but Heather seemed to read her mind.

"Sorry—there's only room for Billy's, uh, models. They can't take in strays, you know—unless you're modeling just for him."

Kristy nodded her head, understanding now. Nude models, she thought. A tiny shiver went through her, thinking how close she had come to succumbing to Billy's offer. That wouldn't be befitting the actress she planned to become.

"Well, I promise to find something and be out of here quickly as possible," she told Heather.

"Yeah, Billy likes his privacy," Heather said. She paused. "But I think he likes you."

That caught Kristy by surprise. "What?"

"Yeah, I can tell."

"Really?" She hadn't thought so. Billy had seemed to be terse and abrupt.

"Otherwise, he wouldn't have let you stay at all."

Kristy thought about that. Did the handsome stranger really like her? The idea excited her, despite her fears.

Heather said she had to go out on a date and left. Kristy felt awkward, being alone with Billy. She tried to stay invisible so not to annoy him. But he was nice. He invited her to eat with him and chatted with her. She found herself flirting with the man, not only in gratitude but also to see if what Heather said was true. She found him attentive and it made her feel pretty.

"Do you have any advice for me?" she asked at one point. She had volunteered to clean up the kitchen and he leaned up against the counter, watching her.

"Just do what you're doing. You can't give up. It's expensive to live here and you just have to do what you have to in order to survive. The toughest ones make it; the rest go back home."

Kristy vowed to be tough.

Afterward, they sat on the couch—her bed—and talked quietly. Billy's voice was soft and hypnotic. He told her about his childhood and how he got started in Hollywood and she ate up every word. She hoped to learn some clues that would help her make it here.

It grew late and Kristy fought a yawn. Billy glanced at his watch. "Well, I'd better let you get to sleep."

"Thank you so much. You're not going to regret it."

"I know. You'll find something. You really do have a quality about your face. I know men in this town will love you." He stood and she jumped up too. Then he did something surprising: He leaned in and kissed her on the cheek. She beamed and watched him walk down the hall toward his bedroom.

He likes me! she thought.

CHAPTER FIVE

The next day, Billy said he would ask around among his photographer friends for a semi-nude modeling job and Kristy went out to find something—anything—in entertainment, knowing she was now on the clock. With her remaining few dollars, she bought new copies of Variety and the Reporter and scanned the ads. Although there always seemed to be new auditions occurring, she was faced with the same problems: Lots of competition and no portfolio. The latter problem loomed largest. Without a book, she was wasting everyone's time.

When she came trudging back to the apartment hours later and was let in by Heather, she relayed her frustrations.

"Everyone's gonna want some shots of me! I really need to get a book put together," she told her friend, already using the jargon of the industry.

"Yeah. Even some simple face shots would get you started."

"I know! How much do you think that'll cost?"

"Hmm. A typical set of shots, showing you in various roles or poses can run up to five hundred, I would think," Heather told her. Kristy's heart sank. "But you might be able to get away with just a basic face shot for a hundred or so."

"A hundred?" Even that amount seemed out of reach.

"But I wouldn't have any shots taken until you get your hair done."

Kristy was startled by Heather's comment. "What's wrong with my hair?"

"Nothing, if you want to stay a farm girl. You look wholesome and sweet and all. But in Hollywood, you gotta look glamorous. Hey, don't look at me that way—it's not an insult."

"What do you think I should do with it? Maybe I could do it myself."

Heather laughed. "Oh no—you're going to need a professional. Someone who can really make you look like a star. Not just a cut, but lighten it up a bit. You know what I mean? Only then do you want to have photos taken."

As Kristy tried to figure out how she might afford all that, Billy returned home. "How're my girls doing?" he joked and Kristy smiled broadly at him. Her cheek stilled burned where he had kissed her. She had never said anything to Heather about it.

Heather volunteered Kristy's problem about lack of photos and she was grateful—she would have been too shy to bring it up.

"No book, huh?" Billy said. "That sucks."

"Do you know of anyone who might help her out? Like on credit?" Heather asked.

Kristy held her breath.

Billy chuckled. "This town isn't known for its generosity, I'm afraid." He turned to Kristy. "You got anything you can trade? Some jewelry or something?"

Kristy shook her head. She remembered her mom's jewelry and wished she had stolen some of it when she had fled. It would've served her right.

"Did you ask any of your friends about doing some modeling?" she asked.

"Yeah. But nothing's doing right now. There's a guy who has a catalog shoot—lingerie and stuff—in a week or so. He said he might be able to use a new face, providing she's got good tits."

The crude language made Kristy's ears burn, but she said nothing.

"I told him about you and he seemed interested."

"That won't help her now," Heather pointed out.

Billy turned on her. "Yeah, well, I'm doing the best I can. I offered her an easy three hundred, but she doesn't want it."

Fear gripped Kristy and she saw just how precarious her position was. "I'm sorry, Billy. I'll find something tomorrow. I promise."

He softened. "No, I'm sorry. I didn't mean to yell. I know you're trying." He paused. "Hey, why don't you show me your resume? Let me see if I can give you some pointers."

"Really? That would be great!" Kristy found a copy in her bag and brought it over. The pages had become little wrinkled, so she smoothed them out on her knee.

Billy raised an eyebrow but said nothing. He took the pages and scanned it quickly. He glanced over at Heather. "Did you see this?"

"No, she never showed me."

He turned to Kristy. "Let me see if I can put this delicately.... This sucks."

Kristy felt her face burn. "What?"

"I'm sorry—I'm just tellin' it like it is. You got two high school productions—that's it?"

"Well, I'm only eighteen!"

He nodded. "Of course. I'm sorry. I don't mean to jump all over ya. I'm just sayin', in this town, a couple of high school plays won't cut it."

"But, uh, what about the commercial? And the pageant?" She was afraid to tell him she lied. She wanted to see how he'd react.

He nodded. "Those are better, yes, if you want to get gigs doing commercials. That's small-time shit. If you go to an audition, they're goin' to want to know that if they hire you, you won't waste their time."

"Uh…"

"You see, movies cost a fortune to make. And when you get an actor who sounds wooden, it ruins the whole movie. Might as well send it direct to video."

"But I don't have any other experience!"

"Have you considered acting lessons?"

"Well, sure, but I can't afford that right now."

"It's the chicken or the egg problem—I see it all the time. Girls come to town without experience and expect to land a big role. Never happens. Oh, they might get a gig or two, here and there, but no casting director's gonna take a chance on an unknown, unless you really wow 'em at the audition. And the ones who do that are usually experienced or have had lots of acting lessons."

"But aren't there people who have natural talent?"

Billy smiled. "Sure. But they're pretty rare. I'm not sayin' you aren't one—I'm just sayin' you got an uphill climb."

"What else can I do? I don't have all that stuff I need! And I need to find something!"

He turned back to Heather. "Whaddya think, Heather?"

She shrugged. "I think she's worth it. She needs a new hairstyle too. Something lighter, more glamorous. It won't be cheap, for everything, I mean."

"I don't know…"

Heather glanced at Kristy and flashed her a supportive smile. "Come on, Billy! She's got a certain something to her. Just look at her face, her body."

Kristy looked from one to the other, confused. "What?"

Billy told her, "This is your lucky day. I don't normally do this, but if Heather believes in you, then I'd say you're worth the risk."

"What?" She felt her heart beating.

"I'm going to invest in you. You know what that means?"

"Not really."

"It means I'll front you the money to get your hair done, the photos and a new resume. We'll just add it to the cost of you staying here. It means I'm into you a few hundred dollars—money I expect will be paid back!"

Her heart leapt. "You'd do that for me?"

He nodded. "It's a loan, right. I'll add it to your total. You'll have to pay me back as soon as you can."

She nodded, her face alight. "Oh thank you! Thank you!" She wanted to hug him but dared not. "How can I ever repay you?"

"Oh, you'll repay me. Trust me."

"Let me make you some dinner. I can cook."

He nodded and she went into the kitchen. He didn't have a lot of food so she volunteered to run to the store, which was just down the block from the apartment. He gave her a twenty and she left.

* * *

When she had gone, Billy turned to Heather. "How'd I do?"

"You did great. You're handling her just right."

He smiled. "Shit. I can't wait to get her out on the street. That fresh-off-the-farm look? She'll make me a fortune." He checked his watch. "Speaking of which…"

"Aw, are you sure you don't want me to stick around, help out with Kristy?"

He shook his head. "You don't think I can handle a stupid farm girl?"

Heather backed down at once. "You gonna be able to explain to Kristy why I'm gone nearly every night?"

He laughed. "Don't worry. That's the easy part."

Heather went to her room to put on her outfit for the night. She slipped out the door before Kristy came home and went downstairs to get Ronald.

* * *

Kristy returned with chicken, vegetables and rice. She rang up and Billy let her into the building. When she entered the apartment, she seemed surprised that Heather wouldn't be joining them.

"Nah, she had to go out. Said she had a hot date."

"Oh." Kristy felt that same uneasiness, as if she were alone with a wild animal. She was attracted to Billy, but she also realized he could rape her if he wanted to and she couldn't do much about it. Hiding her nervousness, she went into the kitchen and started dinner.

"My mom taught me to cook," she said, while Billy fixed them both a drink. He placed the cocktail on the counter in front of her and she took a sip gratefully, glad to be able to calm her nerves. She coughed, not used to strong liquor and pretended she could handle it.

Billy seemed to be on his best behavior. It was like the previous night, when they had chatted about many things. He made them another drink. After a while, Kristy began to lower her guard.

By the time dinner was ready, she was feeling pretty tipsy. He was too. She pulled the baked chicken out of the oven and placed it on the counter and stood back. "Tah-dah!" she said proudly.

Billy came forward. "Wow, looks delicious!" He turned and gave her a big hug. She squealed and tried to pull away but he was too strong. He held her in his grasp and she felt his hardness between his legs. It made her weak. He let her go and said, "Hey, let's eat."

She bustled about putting dinner on the table while he opened a bottle of wine. During dinner, he complimented her on her cooking and she blushed. "Aw, this was nothing," she said. But she felt very proud of herself. She felt lucky to have found Heather and Billy. She pictured herself standing at some future podium, accepting an award and telling the crowd, "I wouldn't be here if it weren't for my friends, Heather and Billy, who took me in when I was just a poor dumb girl fresh off the bus from Indiana." She could hear the applause in her mind.

After dinner, she cleaned up and he poured them two more glasses of wine. "Oh, I don't know if I should! I've got to be fresh for tomorrow!"

"Yeah, I'll call Freddy. That's my photographer friend. He'll set you up with a nice book."

"Thanks again. I will repay you, I promise."

"I know you will." He studied her for a moment, tipping his head sideways.

"What?" She took another sip of wine to mask her nervousness.

"Hmm. I was just picturing you as a blonde. I think you'd look really good."

She straightened up. "Really?"

"Have you ever tried it? I mean, back home?"

"Not really. I did put some highlights in it a couple years ago. Everyone said it looked good. But that was just for the summer." She had done the highlighting herself because she couldn't afford a hairdresser but thought it had turned out okay.

"I really think with your face coloring and body, you'd stand out better."

"Well, if you think so."

"Yeah. I'll ask Freddie to set it all up."

He put his wine down and leaned in and kissed her. It took her by surprise. But his lips were soft and inviting and she found herself swooning. No one had ever kissed her like that before. Billy was so strong and virile. A real man's man. Not like those boys back home, all geeky and fumbling. Or her dad. She suddenly stiffened as a memory of her dad touching her surfaced.

Billy pulled away. "What's wrong?"

"Nothing. I just got a little nervous, that's all."

"Sure." He held her close and she felt better.

"I'm sorry. I don't mean to be a baby."

"It's all right. Everything just seems new and a bit scary to you, doesn't it?"

She nodded in his arms, feeling comforted. His hands rubbed her back. This time, when he bent down to kiss her, she responded. She could feel his kiss all the way to her toes. Kissing him back, she felt one of his hands move around to her front and caress her breasts. The image of her dad surfaced again and she fought it back. No way was she going to be a prisoner of her memories. She was in Hollywood now, a million miles from home. Let the past remain in the past. She kissed Billy again and let his hand rub her breast, her nipple hardening against his palm.

Kristy liked Billy, but more importantly, she knew she had to stay on his good side if she wanted to remain there a few more days. That made it easy to respond to his touch. His hand began unbuttoning the buttons of her blouse and she let him. He was eager and part of her felt glad that he wanted her. It helped quiet that voice inside of her that said she was moving too fast, that she shouldn't be doing this.

But when he leaned down and began kissing the curve of her breasts above her bra line, Kristy began to lose control. Her body shuddered with desire and she suddenly wanted this big strong man. She wanted to be held and caressed and taken. When his hands went to her jeans, she helped him strip her. He lay over her, fully dressed, while she had on just her bra and panties. They grappled together, his hands all over her, his lips on her breasts, neck and face. She felt her bra strap loosen and it fell away, exposing her breasts to him for the first time. Any shyness she may have had was gone under his onslaught of kisses. His fingers pinched her nipples and she giggled.

He spent several long minutes kissing her, caressing her. How could this be wrong? He was so gentle. He murmured how beautiful she was, how sexy, and Kristy swooned. She had to come two thousand miles to find romance and it had just fallen into her lap, unexpectedly. Her hands went over his chest and felt his powerful arms. God! He made her so wet!

His hands slipped down to his pants and Kristy watched, her mouth half open, her breath shallow. He fumbled with his belt and zipper and his hard cock sprang out like a wild animal. Her heart beat faster and she thought she might swoon. Memories of her dad tried to invade her thoughts and she found it easy to push them away. This wasn't dad. Billy was young and strong and virile. A man's man. Not an overweight, abusive slob like her father. This is what a lover should look like.

Without thinking, she found her hand reaching out for his cock and he nodded, encouraging her. "Yeah, baby, that feels good," he said.

"It's so big," she breathed.

"Not too big, I hope." His voice was light.

Truth was, Kristy had only one other penis to compare it to. She hadn't been allowed to date much—her father had had tried to keep her for himself. And his half-flaccid penis had been an object of torment, not love.

"No," she said. "It's nice." She fought her own demons as she gazed upon it.

"Have you touched one before?"

"Yes," she said at once, "I'm not *that* naïve."

He chuckled. "Just checking. Some of you farm girls lead sheltered lives."

I'm not a farm girl, she started to say and decided against it. To Billy, she probably seemed that way, coming from a tame Evansville to big, bad Hollywood. "I wasn't that sheltered."

"Good. 'Cause you need to become street smart to survive in this town."

She nodded, but her concentration was on the erect penis in her hand. It was firm and hard. She could imagine what it would feel like, sliding into her. She shivered.

"You cold?"

"No."

She took her hand off his cock, her nerves returning. He seemed to understand because he didn't say anything that would embarrass her. Instead, he leaned down and began kissing her nipples again. Oh! That felt so good. She hardly noticed when his hands began to slide her panties from her hips. She found herself lifting up to help him. Her body seemed to vibrate at his touch. He pulled them down her legs and tossed them on the floor.

Now she was completely naked and he was almost dressed, except for his unbuckled pants. She reached out and started unbuttoning his shirt and he smiled at her. When the sides came open, he shrugged it off and tossed it on the floor. His torso was magnificent—triangle-shaped and muscular, with a flat stomach and rippling arms.

His hand came around her neck and pulled her toward him. She thought he wanted to kiss her but quickly realized he was aiming her toward his hard cock. Kristy knew all about pleasing a man—her father had given her patient instructions over the years. But his cock had been weak and tiny compared to Billy's monster. It made it easier to push aside bad thoughts and do what she knew how to do so well. His cock barely fit into her mouth and Kristy had trouble remembering her technique. But she must've been doing something right for he began to gasp and moan. She worked harder, expecting him to squirt suddenly into her mouth like her father always did. But he managed to hold off.

"Stop, stop," he said.

She pulled away, puzzled. "What? Was I doing it wrong?"

"Not at all—you're too good! I want to save it."

Her mouth made a little O of understanding and smiled.

Billy eased down her body and she gasped, for it was apparent what he was about to do. It had been something her father had enjoyed and it had always shamed her because she had not been able to keep her body from responding to it.

"Please," she said, but he ignored her. His lips kissed her downy mound and his tongue snaked out and licked at the wetness below. Kristy closed her eyes and tried not to think about her father. That bastard. Why was he still tormenting her, even now? Her body jerked in response to Billy's teasing and she closed her eyes, only to see the top of her father's balding head in her mind. She opened them at once and reached down to pull Billy's head up.

"Please," she said again.

He looked up. "Don't you like this?"

"It's not that. It's..." She couldn't explain. How can anyone understand the images that tortured her?

He seemed puzzled. "What? You can tell me."

"No. I can't." She felt tears come to her eyes and she angrily wiped them away. Damn him! Damn her father for ruining this moment!

Billy eased up over her and rested his body against hers. Kristy could feel his hardness pressing against her clit and it excited her. At least her father hadn't fucked her, she thought, or he might've ruined that too. Suddenly, she wanted this man to take her and flush out all those bad memories. She clung to him and rubbed her pubic bone against him, encouraging him.

He smiled and pushed his pants down so he wouldn't scrap her. She felt the head of his cock slip into her and she gasped and whispered, "I'm not on the pill or anything."

Billy was such a gentleman! He pulled out at once and said, "Thanks for telling me. I should've asked." He reached into the pocket of his jeans and pulled out a condom. Kristy was surprised that he was so well prepared. He slipped it on expertly with one hand and his cock returned to her slippery core.

"Oh god," she whispered as she felt it press inside. He immediately hit her virginal barrier. He pulled back, surprised.

"You're a virgin?"

She nodded, feeling more tears spill from her eyes.

"Are you sure you want to do this?"

"Yes," she said. "Yes." It was past time, she decided. She wanted to be a woman at last. Kristy tugged at him and he pressed himself back into her. She hoped she would know what to do, how to react. She fought her fears as he began to press harder. Her barrier ripped and a sharp pain rippled through her and was gone, just like that. She gasped and held him closer. He began to move and another, smaller pinch radiated out and then she felt a warmth spreading through her.

"Oh!"

"Feels good?"

"Yes!"

He began to fuck her in earnest now, his body rocking hers with each stroke. Kristy felt like a rag doll in his grip. The pain was forgotten as waves of pure pleasure seeped upward into her chest.

"Oh, oh..."

"You're beautiful, baby, beautiful," he murmured.

She could feel it now, that familiar warmth spreading out, bringing her higher and higher. It was vastly different than the ones she had experienced with her father or by her own hand. Those had seemed localized somehow. But this, this was a whole body experience. Even her scalp felt it.

"Oh! Oh! Oh!"

"That's it, baby, come for me, come for me." He was pounding her, his hard cock thrusting deep and Kristy loved it. She wanted to feel his cock spurt inside her and she felt deliciously nasty.

"Yes, yes, yes! Oh god! Oh my god!" She erupted, losing all control and still he fucked her. She came down and immediately started up again toward another climax.

"Oh Billy! Oh! Oh! OH! OH! OH MY GOD!" She erupted again and at the same time, she felt his cock stiffen inside her and throb, once, twice, three times. Heat spread out from her womb and she clung to him as her body shook with her release.

Kristy hugged him closely to her for a long time before she let him go. He pulled back and looked down at her. "That was great," he said. "You are a wonderful lover."

"Th-thank you," she whispered, feeling both pleased and a little shocked at her behavior. She had just fucked a man for the first time! Lost her virginity! Her mind flashed back to Ray, back home, a nice kid who had dated her a few times, despite her disapproving dad. He had kissed her and touched her breasts and she had wanted to go further, just to see what it would be like. But her dad had run him off before it had gotten that far.

So now she knew! And it was wonderful. Wonderful because she had done it with the right man—an experienced man who knew what he was doing. Kristy had no illusions that they would get married. She barely knew Billy. She had wanted to become a sophisticated big-city girl and this seemed to be a shortcut.

And the best part was, her father was nowhere in her mind now. Not after being made love to like that!

Billy pulled back and tossed his condom in the trash. He tugged his pants into position. When he slipped his shirt on, she felt suddenly embarrassed to be naked. Kristy tried to get up and put on her clothes, but he wouldn't let her. "No, I like to see you naked."

She blushed. "But...You're almost dressed."

"Yes." He pushed her back down and kissed her bare breasts. She wondered if he would make love to her again. Her body trembled.

Billy suddenly pulled out his cell phone and aimed it at her. She was startled by the flash and gasped. She sat up and covered her breasts. "What are you doing!?"

"Just taking a picture to remember you by." He held it out and she could see her naked body, spread out obscenely.

"No! You have to erase that!" She reached for his phone and he slapped her hand away.

"Nuh uh. I want to look at this every day and then come home and make love to you all over again."

Kristy felt the heat rise in her chest and felt flattered despite her fear. "You're not going to show that to anyone, are you?"

"Of course not," he said. "Now, tell me what was going on when I went down on you."

His crude talk and sudden segue shocked her. Embarrassment washed through her. The picture was forgotten. She couldn't talk about her father! He wouldn't understand. She tried to make up a convincing lie. "Uh, I just never have let anyone do that," she lied. "It seems, uh, ookie."

He laughed. "Ookie? I haven't heard that one before."

"I guess I seem pretty naïve after all."

"Well, you're young. But I'm telling you, girls love that. Especially the way I do it." He winked. "I want you to let me—but later, okay? I just want you to know that I want to and I won't take no for an answer. I mean, you were pretty good doing it to me."

She blushed. "Uh…"

"Let me guess—back home, you'd give the boys a BJ so they wouldn't try to fuck you, right?"

"Uh, right," she lied again, not wanting him to know the truth. He would think she was weird or damaged.

"Well, just be ready, 'cause it's gonna happen." He reached down and tugged at her hair. "Oh, and start shaving this. When I go down on a girl, I like it clean."

"What?" She had heard of that, of course. Some of the girls at home had done it—she could see them in the showers. But she never thought it was proper.

"You heard me." He gave her a playful slap on her hip and she jumped.

"Now, I'd better let you get ready for bed. Big day tomorrow, right?" He stood up.

"Right." She sat up and was embarrassed to see some blood mixed in with the fluids on the white leatherette cushions. "Oh!"

He noticed and said, "Don't worry. That'll wipe right off." He grabbed some tissues from the coffee table and handed them to her. She quickly cleaned up the evidence of her deflowering. She felt a twinge of sadness that she hadn't saved herself for her future husband, but it probably didn't matter. Few girls did that any more today.

"Well, I'm going to bed. You can use the bathroom down the hall. You'll be all right?"

Kristy had thought for a moment she would be invited into his bed and fought her disappointment. "Uh, yeah. Sure."

He left her there, naked and feeling a bit let down.

CHAPTER SIX

When Heather came stumbling out at noon, Billy was fully dressed and sitting on the couch reading the paper. She looked around.

"Where's Kristy?"

Billy looked up. "I sent her out to get her portfolio done—and her hair too."

Heather nodded. She'd come back owing him a few hundred dollars and Billy would have just the perfect way she could repay him.

"How did it go last night?" Heather knew how Billy operated. Last night should've been his "bonding experience"—i.e., fucking her brains out.

He smiled broadly. "It went well. You wanna see?"

She shrugged. "Sure." She came forward and he showed her the image on his cell phone.

"Nice tits. Is she in looove now?" she asked, stretching the word out for emphasis.

"Maybe. She's got some funny ideas, though."

"What do you mean, funny?"

"Well, she was a virgin, but that didn't stop her. And she was a whiz at cock-sucking! But when I tried to return the favor, she got all weird on me."

Heather felt a stab of memory. "Ah. I thought so."

"What do you mean?"

"She's been abused. Maybe a stepfather or uncle. He taught her how to suck cock and probably brought her off despite herself by going down on her. But they never fucked."

"Then why did she so eagerly suck my dick?"

"'Cause that's what she knew how to do well. She was trying to impress you. But when you went down on her, it probably brought up old memories."

Billy nodded. "Huh. Makes sense."

"Might make it harder to turn her, you know."

"I got no time for that." He shook his head. "I'm sure she'll get over it once the desperation sets in."

"Yeah, you're probably right about that."

"Ronald tells me you had a good night."

Heather nodded. "Nineteen hundred."

"Maybe I'll have to raise your quota."

She frowned but didn't say anything. She knew better than to whine or he'd make it happen. If she just looked pained, he might let her slide. She couldn't bring in that much every night! Changing the subject, Heather asked, "So phase two is beginning now?"

He grinned. "Yep. That girl's not gonna know what hit her."

Heather remembered when Billy had made love to her like that. Every night for nearly a week, he had fucked her until her head spun and she had been lost to his power over her. It had been overwhelming—she thought he loved her and he probably did in a way. So when he had asked for a "small favor" she had been willing to help him out. Soon it would be Kristy's turn.

"Guess I'd better make myself scarce, huh?"

"Yep. I expect you'll be busy earning me big bucks anyway."

"Can't I get a night off?" she found herself asking. "I earned good enough to get a break, didn't I?"

His face darkened. "You don't tell me when you need a break—I tell you!"

"Hey, I was just asking, Billy." She flashed him a thin smile. "I get kinda tired, ya know."

"Ha! You think it's easy, training all these new girls? Shee-it, bitch, you got it made! All you gotta do is spread your legs! I'm the one that's gotta keep everything running smoothly!" His hand went to his belt and she backed off immediately.

"Okay, okay! Forget I mentioned it!"

His mood calmed down. "Okay. But next time you bitch, I'm gonna hafta whip your ass. And just for complainin', I'm telling Ronald to have you out on the corner at six tonight. I want another nineteen-hundred dollar day—at least."

Heather groaned inwardly but kept her face neutral. "Okay." She got up and went into the kitchen to find something to eat.

When Kristy came home at four, Heather let her in and stared at her newly blond hair.

"Wow! It looks great! Makes you look much more sexy!"

"You think so?" She touched her hair. "I thought it was a bit much. I told them just to go up one shade—or put highlights in it. But Freddie insisted."

"Well, he knows best what plays well in this town."

"I guess."

"Well, I'd love to stay and chat, but I've got to run some errands."

"Aww, do you have to? I just got home!"

"Yeah, I'm sorry. And I have a photo shoot later, so I won't get home till late. But I'll see you tomorrow morning. Hey, how did your shoot go?"

"It was great! I saw some of the shots, they looked pretty good!" Her face fell. "But he said he wouldn't be able to print me up something for a couple days! I begged him but he said he had stuff backed up."

"Aw, too bad. But that's not surprising." She gave Kristy a quick hug and said, "Well, gotta go. See ya later!"

Kristy went in and sat on the couch. Billy was gone and she was alone now. She got up and walked around, pretending this was her place. She had just won a big role in a movie and had been paid a couple million. So she had run out and found this place the same day. *It could happen,* she told herself. *I could own a place like this.*

She strolled around, thinking about having a party here, with all her Hollywood friends. Heather would be there, and Billy. Maybe Billy would be her boyfriend and the paparazzi would snap their pictures every time they went out. She went to the mirror in the bathroom and stared at her new look. It did look sexy, she noted. Maybe a little too sexy. But that's what Hollywood is all about, she told herself. Sex sells and she needed to update her image to compete.

She remembered the look on the photographer's face when she had shown up for her appointment. Billy had set it all up. "Just do what he says. He's a pro," he had told her.

Freddie had sent her down the block to a hairstylist he recommended. Kristy had been surprised that the hairdresser could see her right away. Everything had happened so fast! She had been shocked by the new look but Freddie had loved it.

She had to admit that the images she had seen on the back of the camera had been stunning. She looked completely different and not at all like a girl from a rural town in the Midwest. He had also done some in black and white that made her look like a starlet from the '40s and '50s.

"Those are perfect for anyone casting a period movie," he had told her.

Kristy went to the balcony and stepped out. "Hollywood, I'm gaining on you!" she crowed, feeling really happy for the first time since she had arrived in town. She had a good friend in Heather and a wonderful lover in Billy. Who could ask for more?

She heard someone call her name and turned to see Billy coming in. She practically ran into his arms. He hugged her and held her at arm's length, staring at her hair.

"You look great! Very sexy!"

"You think so? I was worried that I might look, you know, too sleazy."

"No, not at all. You gotta remember you're in Hollywood now."

"That's what I've been telling myself."

"How about the resume? Did Freddie help you with that too?"

"Yes! He gave me the name of a friend. Tom something. I'm supposed to see him tomorrow."

"Great!" Suddenly, he frowned. "Hey, did he say how much this all is gonna cost?"

Kristy felt a stab of fear. "Uh, I don't know. I thought you'd know."

He shook his head. "Well, no matter. We'll work it out. I just don't want to get in too deep, you understand. Money has been a little tight lately."

"Oh, really? I'm sorry...I..."

"I'll talk to Freddie, see what's what. Don't worry about it."

He hugged her and ran his hands over her body. She shivered and suddenly wanted to make love again, let her new sexy side come out. He didn't disappoint.

"Come on, let's fool around."

She blushed and followed him to the couch. She was surprised—she expected he'd want to make love to her in his bed, but she didn't argue. He stripped off her clothes and, like before, kept his on. She lay back on the couch and he admired her body.

Suddenly, he reached out and tugged at her hair between her legs. "Hey, I thought I told you to shave this," he said, his voice light but with steel underneath.

"Uh...I haven't had time." That wasn't exactly true. She had been embarrassed to shave her most private part. It would be exposing herself somehow and modesty prevented it.

He gave her a quick slap across her breast and she jerked. "Ow!"

"Next time, I'll really spank you," he said teasingly, although Kristy wasn't sure if he was kidding.

"Okay, okay," she said.

"Good. Now let me look at you." He spent a long time gazing at her and it made her uncomfortable. She started to squirm.

"Hey, relax. You have a beautiful body, you know. You could make a fortune with this."

That wasn't what Kristy wanted to hear. "I want to be an actress."

"Of course. And actresses use their bodies all the time or didn't you know that?"

"Not nude like this!"

He laughed. "Oh? You think you've never seen Angelina Jolie nude? Or Sharon Stone? Halle Barry?"

"Well, yeah, I guess..."

"You're just speaking from old-fashioned Midwestern values. You have to remember that it's different out here."

"I guess it'll take a while to get used to it all."

"That's right. So just go with it. Don't worry so much."

He bent down and kissed her breast and she shivered. His lips roamed over her body and when he went down to her pussy she tried not to think of her father. Fortunately, he didn't linger. Soon he was back kissing her face, her lips, using his hands to inflame her.

"Come on," he breathed. "I want to feel that talented mouth of yours again."

She eagerly went down and unzipped him. His cock was hard and she took him inside. He groaned in appreciation. It was so easy to make a man come, she had learned. Would he stop her this time and fuck her? She slowed down to give him a chance to speak up.

"No, no, keep going," he gasped.

She redoubled her efforts. In a few minutes, she could tell he was close. She squeezed the base of his shaft and tickled his balls and Billy erupted into her mouth.

"Oh, jeez! Oh yes!"

She swallowed his seed and sat back, pleased with herself. She hoped he'd be able to recover enough to fuck her now. Her pussy throbbed with need.

But he simply zipped up his pants and patted her head. "Thanks."

Her mouth dropped open but she didn't say anything. She just watched as he went to the kitchen to find himself a beer.

"You want one?"

"Uh, no, no thanks." She lay sprawled there, still naked and waited for some kind of direction from Billy. He returned, sipping his beer and she shook her head.

"What's wrong?"

"Nothing. I just thought..."

"Oh, that we'd fuck? We will. You gotta give me some time to recover. You really know how to give a guy a great blowjob!"

She felt flattered but still confused. She reached for her clothes. He put his hand out to stop her.

"Nah, I want you to stay naked. It'll get me back in the mood sooner. You want to fuck, dontcha?"

Kristy paused. She felt uncomfortable, being naked. She tried to tell herself she was just being a rube and she should get over it. Taking a breath, she nodded. "Okay."

"Good!" He took another sip of his beer. "Walk around for me. I like to see you move, especially in that new hair."

Kristy got up and on shaky legs, walked around in front of Billy as he encouraged her. Her skin felt hot and she couldn't stop blushing. But after a few minutes, she did notice it became easier. After all, it was just her and Billy in the room. It wasn't like Heather was watching her or anything!

His cell phone rang and he answered it. "Yeah?" His face darkened. "Really? You're shittin' me."

Kristy wondered what news caused his sudden change of mood. She waited, her arms crossed in front.

"That wasn't the deal," he barked into the phone. "Well, shit..." He hung up. He stared at Kristy and she suddenly felt very naked. She hunched down under his gaze.

"That was Freddie. He called to give me the bill for today."

"What?" She thought it had all been worked out. Something about favors owed...

"He said the shoot and the hairdresser came to a total of four hundred fifty dollars!" His voice had an ugly edge to it. "Four hundred fifty dollars!"

Kristy shrank before him and sat down on a chair across from the couch. "I didn't know. They didn't tell me it was that much!"

"I expected one-fifty for the shoot. I thought he had some kinda deal worked out with the hairdresser, but no! Now, with the fifty bucks you owe me for staying here tonight, that's gonna be five hundred! And I have no idea what Tom's gonna charge for the new resume."

Kristy was shocked. Weren't they lovers now? Why would he worry about a few lousy hundred dollars? "I can pay you back," she told him. "With all this help you've given me, I can certainly get a job now."

He nodded and his tone softened, just like a switch being turned off. "I'm sorry. You're right. When can you go out and start circulating your resume and photos?"

Kristy felt her stomach lurch. "Uh...I don't think a new resume will take very long. But Freddie said the photos won't be ready for a couple days. Something about him being all backed up."

His face went still. "Shit."

"I'm sorry. Do you want me to go?"

"And where would you go? No, you have to stay here now. I've invested too much in you."

She nodded. That had been her thinking. Except she had hoped she was worth more to him than just a few lousy hundred bucks. He was her lover!

"Tell ya what," he said suddenly. She gave him her full attention. "I know you don't want to keep racking up charges, so I'll make you a deal, okay?"

"Uh, sure..."

"I love looking at you. You have a great body. It's a like a piece of art, you know?"

Kristy beamed with pride.

"So here's the deal—if you'll agree to walk around nude, I'll let you slide for a few more days on what you owe me."

"What?!" Her mouth dropped open.

"Yeah. Unless you got a better place lined up."

"No, but...I can't! Heather would see me!"

"Oh, Heather's seen naked girls before, trust me! And she's posed naked too, so it's nothing to her. You worry too much."

"I can't! I just can't!"

"You'd rather pay me the five hundred now?"

Kristy thought fast. He was being so mean! Why did he have to demand she be naked! It was so embarrassing! "Please...I don't know what to do!"

He came forward and helped her to her feet and wrapped his arms around her. "There, there, I know it sounds weird. I just love seeing you naked. Especially those tits! I thought it was a way you could really cut your expenses. It would be a win-win. Besides, if you were naked, you'd get a lot more lovin'."

She felt a shiver run through her and her pussy twitched with need. She found herself nodding, although she still wasn't entirely convinced.

"Tell ya what. Go into the bathroom and shower and shave that sweet pussy of yours for me. When you come out, you'll see a robe of Heather's on the back of the door you can wear for a while, okay?"

She nodded dreamily, enjoying the feel of his arms around her. She tried not to think about what he was asking of her. He pulled away and turned her sidewalks and gave her a sharp slap on her bottom to shake her out of her reverie.

"Now go, my sweet girl."

Kristy went. She showered and shaved, feeling strange about it, but doing it anyway. When she looked down, she appeared to be a pre-teen again. Why did he want that? Was it a particular fetish of his? As long as it pleased him, she was happy to do it, she decided. She owed him so much! She dried off and put on the short silk robe of Heather's. It was a pale blue and came just to mid-thigh. She felt almost naked wearing it, but it was better than being completely naked!

She hadn't washed her hair, so she shook it out and combed it, trying to remember how the hairdresser had done it. As she tipped her head this way and that, she had to admit, she did look a lot more like a movie star.

She came out and Billy smiled and said, "Turn around, baby. That robe looks good on you."

She blushed and turned, wigging her hips a bit.

"Did you do as I asked?"

Kristy nodded. "Yeah." Her voice was small.

"Well, show me!"

Fighting her embarrassment, she undid the sash and opened her robe. She tried to close it just as quickly, but Billy held up his hand. "No, baby, let me see you. You know I love your body."

She wanted to be loved for more than her body, but she did as he asked, holding her robe open so he could see her newly shaved pussy. She felt her face grow red.

"Don't be shy, Kristy," he said softly. "You have to get used to showing off, you know? I mean, it's good training for your acting. Someday, you may be asked to make love to Brad Pitt and then where would you be if you got all weird on him?"

She nodded and tried to imagine that day but she couldn't. She'd be lucky if she got a movie role opposite Rob Schneider.

"Come here."

Kristy approached and Billy's hands were on her, inflaming her. The robe fell away and she soon forgot about her nakedness.

All she thought about was Billy's cock and how it would feel inside her.

He eased her down onto the couch and she responded to him, eager to please him and not just because she owed him so much. She imagined herself as his girlfriend now. Sure, it was an unusual relationship, but this is how things were done in Hollywood. She had to keep telling herself that.

Billy went down on her and Kristy watched, fighting her demons. But she had to admit, it did feel different now that she was shaved.

"Oh!"

A sudden wave of pleasure rippled through her.

"Oh!"

Kristy spread her legs apart and settled in. Billy's tongue was very talented! She closed her eyes and tried to keep her mind focused on the present. Whenever the image of her father's bald spot encroached on her thoughts, she opened her eyes to gaze upon Billy's full head of hair and felt better. Within minutes, she no longer had to worry about anything— the sensations were rolling through her and she found herself rocking her hips in rhythm to his tongue.

"God! Oh yes! Yes!"

The orgasm cascaded over her and she went off to another place for a few minutes. When she returned, she found Billy looming over her, his pants unbuckled and his hard cock sticking out. He rubbed the tip against her.

"Condom," she begged.

"I'll pull out," he promised and thrust himself in at once.

She gasped and held on tight. He fucked her hard and fast and she was worried he might come inside. It diminished her pleasure but she wasn't about to say anything. If he got her pregnant, he'd have to deal with it. Maybe he'd marry her and they'd start a family.

His thrusts sped up and she found another orgasm approaching.

"Yeah, baby, you'd my little slut, my cute little whore," he mumbled as he neared his climax.

Kristy tried not to be offended and rode along with him until she could feel her orgasm erupt inside her. As she climaxed, he pulled out and squirted his seed all over her belly and breasts. She gasped with delight and gratitude and hugged Billy close to her.

"Thank you, thank you," she gushed.

"You're very welcome," he said and chuckled softly in her ear.

When they separated, Kristy cleaned herself up with tissues and picked up her robe. Billy tsked at her. She looked up. "Really?"

"Really."

She dropped the robe and tried to get used to being naked. Billy was such a strange man! Sometimes he could be so gentle and loving, and other times he showed his steely side. But she had to admit, he was all man!

Billy made her stay naked all evening while he remained dressed. It took a while, but she eventually got used to it. He seemed so appreciative of her body he could hardly keep his hands off of her. She just wanted a break now and hoped to distract him with food or music. But that proved to be impossible. He seemed drunk with her body and she didn't quite know how to handle it. Yes, it made her feel sexy and alive, but she also thought it was wrong somehow to be paraded about.

When Billy went to bed, she was once again relegated to the couch. She tried to hide her disappointment.

CHAPTER SEVEN

The next morning around nine, she got up, planning to head out once again. She had on Heather's robe and she hoped Heather wouldn't miss it. As she was making coffee, Billy came into the kitchen, dressed only in boxer shorts. He immediately grabbed her shoulder with one hand, spun her about and gave her several sharp slaps on her bottom.

"Ow!"

"Naughty girl," he said teasingly. His hands untied the sash and Kristy allowed the robe to slip off her body. He went into the living room and tossed it over the couch.

"Really? What if Heather sees?"

"Relax," he said, returning to the kitchen. "I told you she's used to it. Besides, she won't be up for awhile."

"Oh, okay. I'll be gone by then."

"Got some more auditions?"

"Uh, something like that." Truth was, she couldn't do anything until she got her book. She planned to buy a new copy of Variety and make some inquiries about modeling.

"How about a quick blowjob before you go?"

"Oh, uh, sure." Kristy felt the heat rise in her face again. She tried to push away those thoughts that told her she was being exploited and remembered how Billy put her up when he didn't have to. She sank to her knees and freed his cock. It was almost second nature to her now. She soon had him gasping. When he came in her mouth, she swallowed it all and smiled up at him.

"You're a great cocksucker," he said.

Kristy felt a grimace fly across her face and tried to conceal it. Why was he saying such crude things to her? She chalked it up to just his nature and tried to smile her way through it.

"I'll make us some breakfast." She got up and went into the kitchen, happy to have something to do that wasn't all about sex. Billy had sex on the brain! Of course, cooking while naked didn't seem to help matters. He came in and wrapped his arms around her as she stood at the stove, frying eggs.

She tried to squirm her way free and said lightly, "Hey, you'll make me burn your breakfast."

"Sorry. I just can't keep my hands off of you."

She made him a plate and was glad to see him sit down at the small table to eat. But he wasn't done with her yet. "Hey, come here and sit next to me."

"What about my breakfast?"

"You can have some of mine. Besides, you don't want to get fat, do ya? You know how tough those casting agents can be."

Kristy frowned. She didn't feel overweight—why would he say such a thing? Did he think she was getting flabby? She looked down at herself.

He laughed. "Hey, I was just kidding! Come here."

She went to him and he made her sit on his lap while he ate. He fed her some bites. A bit of egg yolk dripped on her breast and Billy licked it up, and used the opportunity to suck on her nipple. Kristy squirmed. It felt good, but she felt so exposed!

At that moment, Heather came stumbling around the corner, dressed in an oversized tee-shirt, and headed for the kitchen. Kristy squealed and tried to get up, but Billy held her firmly. Heather smiled at her and nodded, then went past to grab the coffee carafe.

"Billy!" Kristy hissed.

"Relax, Heather knows how I live. Right, Heather?"

Heather came back, coffee cup in hand. "Yeah, don't worry, Kristy. This is nothing." She took a sip and rubbed the sleep from her face.

Their cavalier attitude didn't make Kristy feel any better. "But...but...Please! Let me get dressed!"

Billy ignored her and held her firmly in place. "What are you doing up so early?" he asked Heather.

"I don't know. I just couldn't sleep for some reason. I'll probably take a nap later."

Billy's hand went between Kristy's legs and his fingers began to stroke at her core. Kristy was in no mood to be aroused. She wiggled her hips to express her disapproval. Billy didn't stop.

"Well, maybe you could run an errand for me, then," Billy was saying to Heather, acting casual, as if he had a naked girl on his lap all the time.

"Sure, I guess. Long as it's not too strenuous."

"Oh? Long night?"

"Not too bad. My, uh, modeling assignment finished by midnight. Then Ronald wanted to visit with me for a while. You know, catch up on gossip."

"Right."

Kristy tried to pretend she wasn't there. His fingers had unlocked her wetness, despite her embarrassment and Kristy wanted him to stop even as she wanted him to continue. Finally she stopped struggling and allowed her legs to open a bit wider for his hand.

Billy and Heather talked softly, but it soon became background noise to Kristy. Her attention was focused on his finger, moving between the soft wet folds of her skin, teasing her, making her wetter and more excited. When he shifted his legs to open her up more, she didn't fight him. His other hand snaked up to cup her breast and thumb a nipple. Kristy's mouth fell open and she sagged against his chest.

Heather didn't seem to care that Billy was bringing Kristy off right in front of her and Kristy soon ceased caring as well. Her hips began to move in time with his stroking. An orgasm began to bubble up inside her and she heard herself making little noises in her throat. At that moment, Heather stood up and came close. She leaned down and kissed Kristy on the lips.

Suddenly, before she could react to Heather's outrageous actions, Kristy's climax burst over her and she gasped aloud. "Oh! Oh god!" She trembled in his arms.

"That's what I like to see," Billy said. "A little girl-on-girl action! I'll bet people'd pay a lotta money to see that!"

Kristy felt weak and uncoordinated. Billy picked her up in his powerful arms and brought her to the couch. She lay limply, watching the two of them talk as if she hadn't just climaxed in front of them. They said nothing about the kiss. Why had she done that? Was Heather a lesbian? Or was this just more laid-back California behavior?

As she recovered from her climax, Kristy reached for her robe and draped it across her, trying to cover up. Her embarrassment was returning. Heather noticed at once and said, "So that's where my robe went to!" She came over and pulled it from Kristy's unresisting fingers.

"Yeah, blame me," Billy said. "I let her wear it."

"That's fine—I just thought I'd lost it." She put it on and Kristy shrunk into herself, trying to hide.

"I'm sorry," she said quietly.

"Don't worry about it." She turned to Billy. "Well, I guess I'll go shower, leave you two lovebirds alone." She gave Kristy a knowing wink and left.

Kristy immediately felt less embarrassed. It was one thing to be naked in front of Billy—her lover—and quite another to be naked in front of her new friend Heather! Especially if Heather was gay. Would she want to make love to her sometime? Kristy didn't want to think about that.

Billy joined her on the couch. She tried to get up. "I should get ready to go..." she began.

"Relax! Heather's using the bathroom. Sit with me while I make some phone calls." He pulled out his cell phone and hit a speed dial button. He began to talk to someone about "merchandise" and Kristy found herself tuning out.

Sure enough, Billy's hand snuck over between her legs and began to tease her again. Kristy kept her legs together, for she didn't want to allow herself to be treated like a sex object. She was an actress! But it did feel good. And his fingers were so gentle. His voice droned on. He seemed to have a lot of businesses going on. So successful! And he was nice, letting her stay there for so many days, without asking her to pay until she could afford it. Where would she be without him? So she let her legs come apart again and drifted. Her orgasm took longer to arrive this time.

"Wait a minute, let me write that down," Billy said suddenly into the phone and his hand came away from her pussy. Kristy felt a letdown and said nothing while Billy jotted down some information on a pad on the coffee table. "Got it."

She waited, legs askew until his hand returned. She opened up in greeting and rolled her hips to give him better access. He teased her lightly, never allowing her to climb that stairway to orgasm. Kristy grew frustrated and tried to encourage him. But he was busy with his conversation. When he hung up with one person, he immediately dialed another.

She didn't realize how much time had gone by until Heather came into view suddenly, completely dressed, and Kristy instantly closed her legs, trapping Billy's hand. Heather smiled and waved a hand as if to say, *Relax.*

"I'm gonna go, Billy. What is it you wanted me to do?"

"Oh." Billy's hand came away and Kristy hunched over. "Get Ronald to drive you down to the bus station. I think a friend of mine is coming into town today."

Heather sighed. "Really? You sure?"

"Yeah. Just wait there for a couple hours. You know the drill."

"Yeah, okay." She sighed and headed for the door.

When she left, Billy went back to his phone and his hand returned to Kristy's pussy. She gave up all resistance and spread her legs wide for him. If this is what he wants to do, who was she to deny him? She liked the attention.

Kristy found herself responding to his expert touch. It was weird, listening to him talk to someone while he was stroking her. Like she was a sideline, something to do while he talked business. She supposed it was better than having him doodle. She smiled. He was doodling, in a way—doodling her clit.

"Okay, see ya," Billy said and hung up. He turned to Kristy who was half-gone, her hips shaking as her orgasm rose within her. He pulled his hand away. She groaned at once and opened her eyes to plead with him.

"Hey, you'd better get ready to go, if you want to get a job and all."

That brought her back to earth. "Uh, yeah." She struggled to get to her feet, her pussy still tingling. Why didn't he let her finish? Kristy stood there for a moment, half-expecting him to tell her to sit down so he could bring her off. Wasn't that fair? She brought him off. When he didn't speak, she simply nodded and picked up her robe. He didn't object. She slipped it on and retreated to the bathroom.

When she came out, forty-five minutes later, she had on the robe. Kristy planned to grab another cup of coffee and finish getting ready, but when she rounded the corner, she stopped in shock. Billy wasn't alone! He was sitting on the couch across from a good-looking black man. The man smiled when he became aware of her presence and Billy turned to see her. She shrank back to the safety of the hallway.

"Come on, don't be shy, you're covered," Billy said, waving her forward.

Reluctantly, she stepped out into the living room.

"This is Duane, he showed up while you were in the shower. He's an old friend of mine."

Duane stood up, a big smile on his face. He was tall with close-cropped black hair. He seemed about Billy's age, in his early thirties.

"Hi, you must be Kristy," he said, his hand outstretched.

"Uh, yeah." She clutched the robe more tightly around her and sidled forward to shake his hand. "I, uh, just got out of the shower."

"Come, sit," Billy said, patting the couch next to him.

"No—I should get dressed."

"Nonsense. Remember what we talked about," he warned. She shuffled forward and sat, pulling at the edges of her robe to keep herself covered. It was embarrassing!

"Billy tells me you're new in town, want to be a star," Duane was saying.

Kristy had to tear her mind away from her near-naked condition and focus on him. "Yeah."

"What do you want to do? Anything in particular?"

"No, just get a break. Any role will do. Even a commercial."

"Well, Billy here is always looking for models."

"Yeah, we're talking about that," Billy interjected before Kristy could answer. "Kristy here owes me some money, so you could say we're negotiating right now."

"Ohh," Duane said, winking. "Don't let this guy take advantage of you."

"I won't."

Billy hugged her to him and her robe slipped up, exposing more skin. She fought to keep herself decent.

"Hey, relax. You're all tense."

"I should get dressed," she repeated.

"Oh? So you can pay me back then?" His words cut through her and she froze.

"You know I can't, Billy." She glanced up to see Duane's eyes on her body. He looked hungry and she felt like a hunk of meat in a lion's cage.

"Okay then, just relax." He pulled her tighter to him and Kristy noted that the skimpy robe was nearly up to her hips. She kept her legs tightly closed. Billy began rubbing one of her breasts through the silky material, making her nipple stand out despite her embarrassment.

"Now, where were we, D?"

"I was asking you about the deal with Artful Entertainment."

"Oh, right." They began to talk business and Kristy seemed to be forgotten for the moment. But his hands never stopped touching her. Even as they talked, Kristy could see Duane's eyes flicking across her body now and then, watching how she was practically on display for him.

What was worse, Billy's touch began to inflame her, making her squirm, caught between arousal and embarrassment, especially since she hadn't been allowed to climax that last time. Her thoughts became mixed up and she fought to maintain control over her emotions.

She couldn't seem to let go and she began to wiggle in his arms, trying to get away and cover herself up.

"Hey!" Billy's voice cut through her thoughts. "Stop squirming unless you got a few hundred on ya!"

She gave in and allowed his hands to roam over her. She was trapped, dependent on this man to save her from the streets. And he was her lover, after all. The least she could do was not be a crybaby! When his hand gripped her breast and pulled at her robe, she didn't say anything. Her robe rode up and uncovered her now bare pussy. She turned away, her face bright red.

They didn't seem to pay attention—they were still talking about some deal Billy was negotiating. Kristy stared at a corner of the room and tried to make herself invisible. But his fingers were hard to ignore. He pushed aside the material and allowed one of her breasts to flop out. She gasped and tried to cover up. Billy playfully slapped her bare breast and she backed down. Now Duane was looking right at her naked breast and she could do nothing about it. She bit her lip and tried to tell herself this was no different than showing herself off to Heather. Yet it felt vastly different.

Soon, her other breast was exposed and Kristy felt mortified. Billy's hand were stroking her, teasing her, all the while he and Duane talked business. She was nothing more than a diversion, eye candy—an object for Billy to play with. She closed her eyes and wished she were somewhere else.

Suddenly, she felt the couch sink next to her and turned to see Duane there. She shrank back toward Billy and again tried to pull her hemline down to cover up. Billy slapped her thigh and warned, "Be nice. Duane is a friend of mine."

Kristy nodded and sat there in between the two men, wishing she could disappear into the couch. Duane's hand touched her left thigh and began to rub her. She turned to Billy with a question in her eyes and he just nodded as if to say, *He has my permission.*

She couldn't believe it. Why would he do this? Wasn't she *his* girl? She heard her name and she realized they were talking about her, not the deal.

"Kristy here owes me a lot of money. Heather brought her home one day like a stray dog. I let her stay here against my better judgment. You know how once a person moves in with you, it can be hard to move her out again?"

"Yeah, man, I hear ya," Duane said, his fingers moving higher toward the vee of her legs. Her thighs hurt from clamping them together.

She wanted to scream, *But what about the lovemaking? You said I was special! I was your girl, wasn't I?*

Now Billy's hand came down to the sash and untied it. His hand went inside to rest against her stomach.

"Please," she begged.

"Shhh," he said, rubbing her stomach. "Just relax. You're among friends here."

"I'm scared."

"Don't be. I'll always take care of you. You should know that."

Kristy wasn't sure about that. Everything was moving so fast! She had gone from an innocent girl to a made up sexpot who was allowing a strange man to fondle her in less than a week.

"Doesn't it feel good?"

She could only nod, for that was the answer she knew Billy wanted to hear. And it did feel good, in a way. So what if her breasts were exposed? So what if Duane was touching her leg. *This is all because Daddy wouldn't let me date*, she told herself. *Otherwise, I'd be more experienced with all this. And this is better than being thrown into the street.*

Duane's fingers tickled her bare mound and Kristy closed her eyes and gave a soft moan, deep in her throat. It was a moan of fear more than arousal, but Billy jumped on it.

"See, it must feel good."

Billy's hands began thumbing her nipples, making them hard. He pinched them gently and Kristy found it made her legs unclench despite herself. She was opening up to their caresses. Duane took advantage at once, sliding a middle finger down along the incurving line of her vagina. She moaned again and this time, it was more due to arousal than fear.

"That's it, just relax. You're my girl and I like showing you off. You are beautiful." His words quieted the discordant voices inside her. Her pussy twitched under Duane's gentle touch. Her legs came apart imperceptibly and she leaned back against the cushions. She didn't fight Billy when she felt him pull apart the edges of her robe, exposing her naked body to the men's gazes.

If this is what he wants, she thought, and allowed herself to be fondled. She felt the first tendrils of an orgasm begin to form. Her legs sagged open, encouraging the men and their fingers grew bolder. Now Duane's fingers were actively stroking her wet pussy, drawing up moisture to the hard nubbin of flesh where her womanhood resided. Pleasure radiated out from that point and into her breasts, limbs and up into her head.

Billy bent down and began sucking on one of her nipples. She groaned and pulled him more tightly to her. She began jerking her hips as her orgasm bubbled up. Yes, just a few more seconds...

Suddenly, Duane's fingers pulled away. Kristy opened her eyes at once and watched as he got down on his knees in between her legs and roughly pulled them apart. "No, no," she said, memories flooding back. But Duane was not easily dissuaded. His mouth went to her pussy and he began to lick her. God, it felt good—and he didn't remind her at all of her father! His tongue was talented and she struggled for a few seconds to purge her mind of her past images. Then the orgasm that had been hovering out there began to swell within her and she stopped fighting. She held on, thinking only of her pleasure. It rushed through her and she cried out, her hips jerking against Duane's mouth.

"Oh god! Oh god!"

She collapsed against the couch and couldn't move when she felt Billy ease her forward so that he could remove her robe entirely. He tossed it over the back of the couch, leaving her completely naked. She thought she should be embarrassed, but she seemed way past all that.

Billy unbuckled his pants and Kristy sat up in alarm. He wanted to make love to her in front of Duane? Is that how men acted in Hollywood? His cock bobbed into view and Billy didn't seem at all concerned that Duane was right next to her watching. She felt Billy's hand on the back of her neck, tugging her down. She glanced over at Duane and thought, *Well, if this is what Billy wants...*

Her head went down and she took Billy's cock into her mouth. Kristy pushed aside her negative thoughts and made her mind blank. She had one job to do and she didn't want to think too much about it. Billy was excited, she could tell, for his cock began to jerk after just two minutes and he suddenly squirted into her mouth.

"Oh man! That was great!" he bellowed.

She pulled back and he quickly tucked his cock back in his pants. She turned to see Duane smiling at her and she felt embarrassed all over again.

Billy leaned over and whispered into her ear. "I owe Duane two hundred dollars. If you'll agree to be nice to him, he'll waive my debt to me, and I'll subtract two hundred of the money you owe me, okay?"

She tried to sit up, her eyes coming back into focus. "What?"

"Just be nice to Duane. That's all."

Kristy focused on Duane and noticed he was unbuckling his pants. She turned to Billy in alarm. He was getting up.

"Wait!"

"It's an easy way to reduce your debt. It means you can stay here a few more days. Don't you want to stay?"

"Yes, but…"

"Good. Then just be nice to Duane and do what he says." Billy moved away from the couch and Kristy tried to follow him with her eyes, pleading. "But, Billy! How can you…"

"Shh," he said from halfway across the room. "I'll be back in just a few minutes. You'll be fine."

And he was gone down the hallway to his room.

Kristy turned back to see Duane's naked cock jutting out from thick black curls. It was larger than Billy's and she stared at it. She realized she had lived a very sheltered life up until this moment. Now she was being asked to "be nice" to this man in exchange for her right to stay there?

He moved closer and Kristy found herself reaching out for his cock. She knew she had two choices and giving him oral sex seemed to be the lesser of two evils. Although she was aroused, she didn't want to fuck this strange man. The fact that he was black and she had never been around a black man before really wasn't the issue. He was simply a stranger to her. And now she was alone with him and his cock was inches from her mouth.

Kristy bent down and allowed his cock to invade her mouth. It was big and she had to modify her tried-and-true techniques. She felt it swell inside and she nearly choked when he grabbed the back of her head and began to fuck her face. Aligning her throat, Kristy opened up and allowed him to have his way with her. She felt helpless in his strong hands.

He sped up and she thought her ordeal would soon be over. At the last minute, he pulled out and squirted his seed all over her face. She gasped and coughed and felt the slime cover her cheeks.

"Ahh, that's how a white woman should look—covered with a black man's jizz," Duane said.

Kristy's ears burned. She reached up to try to wipe it off, but there was too much of the viscous fluid. It covered her fingers and she rubbed them against her breasts.

At least it's over now. "I'd better go clean up," she said.

"Wait."

She froze.

"Suck me again."

"But you can't possibly..."

"Just do it."

Kristy bent down and took his semi-flaccid cock inside, her mouth already tired. But she did what she was told to do. Her eyes widened in shock when she felt his cock begin to harden. How can he come again, she wondered. Can men do that? She had never experienced it before.

When he was fully hard again and Kristy thought he might give her face another blast, Duane pulled out and roughly pushed her down on her back. He climbed up over her and she gasped when she saw his hard cock aiming toward her pussy.

"Wait! Wait! I can't!"

"Sure you can. You fucked Billy, didnja?"

"No! No! Billy! Billy!"

Duane slapped her breast hard and she gasped and stopped fighting. "Don't be a drag! You're in Hollywood now. You gotta build relationships out here. Someday, I may hire you for a job just because you were nice to me tonight."

That gave her pause. Was he a producer or casting director?

"If it'll make you feel better, I'll wear a condom," he continued, bending down to pull one from his pants. For some reason, it did make her feel better and she accepted this small favor.

The condom slipped over his cock and he steered it toward her pussy. Kristy could do nothing to stop him. She was about to be fucked in exchange for a debt. As his cock slipped inside, she gasped with the size of it inside her. She felt filled up for the first time in her young life. After that, it was all just fucking. She was a rag doll at the end of his magnificent cock. But he wasn't entirely selfish. He was a good lover, making sure she climbed up to two powerful orgasms before he bellowed and came hard and she felt his release.

They sagged apart. Duane got up and pulled the condom off his cock and tossed it into a nearby trash can.

"Thanks, babe." He got dressed quickly and left without another word to her.

Kristy lay sprawled on the couch, still naked, still breathing hard when Billy returned. He smiled down at her. "Now, that wasn't so hard, was it?"

She couldn't move. She just stared at him.

"You just knocked two hundred off your debt. That gives you a little more breathing room. Feels good, doesn't it?"

CHAPTER EIGHT

When Heather rose the next day at noon, she found Billy at his usual place on the couch, sipping a cup of coffee.

"Is the farm girl gone?"

"Yeah," he said, turning to smile at her. "She said went to see Tom about her resume."

"Did she get her portfolio already?"

Billy laughed. "No. Not until tomorrow. Or maybe the next day."

Heather nodded. She knew Billy had asked Freddie to delay her book so he could force her to become more beholding to him.

"How did it go yesterday?"

"Good. Kristy paid off two hundred of her debt."

"Who was the lucky guy?"

"Duane."

Heather would've liked to have seen that. Duane was a good lover. She could remember a similar experience with another one of Billy's friends four years ago, when she had gotten started in the business. Billy had held her debts over her just as he did with Kristy. Not many women chose to go back out on the street when they've had a taste of the good life here in Billy's apartment. Of course, the girls don't get to stay here very long anyway.

"Wish I was around to watch," she said. "Duane's a fine man."

Billy smiled and picked up the remote. "You can watch it, if you want to." He pressed a button and images formed on the TV screen. Heather's eyes widened. She could see Kristy sucking on Duane's cock.

"You filmed it!"

"You bet. Didn't want to miss the good parts."

She watched, mesmerized as Kristy received a face full of come and was ordered to make him hard again. That Duane, he was a marvel. She couldn't tear her eyes away as the farm girl was fucked to two orgasms.

"Wow. Looks like she kinda liked it."

"Oh, she's a sexy bitch, that's for sure." He flicked off the TV.

"Heard you had an off night." His tone carried menace.

"It was raining! No one wants a whore when it's raining! Besides, I was tired from hanging around that bus station half the day for nothing."

Billy chuckled. "Yeah, that's okay. I was just ribbin' ya. I guess you could say I'm in a good mood. I'm glad you brought me Kristy—I think she's gonna be a real money-maker."

Heather breathed a sigh of relief. "I do know how to pick 'em, don't I? You want me to keep looking for another one?"

He shrugged. "Sure. I've got another week or so with Kristy first, so I'll be in the market for a new bitch soon enough. But don't pick up one unless she's as cute as Kristy is, okay?"

* * *

Kristy wandered the streets of Hollywood, despair in her heart. She had just left Tom's small print shop. He had really helped her come up with new language to help flesh out her resume and make her sound like a fledging actress and not a naïve girl from Indiana. Tom printed it up on heavyweight ivory bond and gave her two dozen copies to start. She could have more for a small extra fee. The entire process had taken just ninety minutes, so when he handed her a bill for two hundred dollars to take back to Billy, she had been shocked

"Th-that much?" It sounded outrageous to her. Two hundred for ninety minutes in front of a computer and a few sheets of paper? Yes, the resume looked great, but...

"Sure. That's with a discount for Billy. Normally it'd be closer to three hundred."

She could guess how Billy would react. She still owed the man three-fifty. After handing him Tom's bill, she'd be back to owing five-fifty again! She had few illusions about how she might be paying him back. Kristy felt trapped. Part of her rebelled and told her to just leave—but where would she go? She needed those photos and the resume! If she had those, she could start going on auditions again.

Damn.

The logical part of her brain kicked in. *It wasn't so terrible, was it? I mean, you made love to Billy and you liked it. Duane was nice too. Back in high school, you wanted to date Roy and you would've made love to him if you'd had the chance. So what's the big deal? You traded a quick fuck with a nice guy for two hundred dollars off your debt and the right to stick around a few more days. Billy said he wasn't running a halfway house for runaways, didn't he? He was nice enough to front you the money for your photos, resume and your new hairstyle. Now you're almost there! Don't ruin things by being a baby!*

Feeling a little better, Kristy went down to the newsstand and bought some papers. She sat on a bus bench and scanned through them. Another casting call, this time for a low-budget horror film, was happening tomorrow morning. Maybe the photographer would have her book ready by then. She decided to walk down to his studio and ask.

Walking among the street preachers, drunks and whores didn't bother her as much as it had on her first day, Kristy noted. She kept her eyes focused ahead and never on some of the people who passed by her. She was an island in a sea of craziness.

It took her twenty minutes to walk to the photographer's studio. "Hollywood Fotos by Freddie" the sign said. She went in and spotted the same bored receptionist she remembered from the day before.

"Hi," she said, putting false cheer in her voice. "Remember me? I was here doing a shoot the other day."

The girl glanced up from her romance novel. "Oh, yeah," she said without enthusiasm. Her brown hair hung limply around her face. She was skinny and had two gold rings in her left eyebrow and a tongue stud that Kristy could see when she talked.

"I was wondering if my photos might be done? I have an audition tomorrow morning and I was hoping..."

"No, they aren't done." It was said with flat finality. "He said two-three days, dinnhe?"

"Well, yes, but I hoped..."

"He's busy, you know. Everybody comes in here and wants their shit yesterday. You'll just have to wait." She returned to her book.

Kristy looked around. The waiting room was deserted and it didn't appear Freddie was all that busy. "Can I see him? Freddie?"

The girl looked up, scorn in her expression. "I can't take him away from his shoot just so he can tell you the same thing I'm tellin' ya."

"Oh? Is he shooting someone now?" Kristy listened, but she couldn't hear anything.

"Yeah."

Kristy decided not to alienate this woman further or she might never get her photos. "Could you tell him that Kristy Carnes stopped by and really wants her photos? I could swing by in the morning, say, nine a.m., and pick them up on my way to the audition."

The girl shrugged. "I'll tell him."

Kristy left, shaking her head at the type of people who found jobs in this town. *That girl probably makes ten bucks an hour and has no chance for a career in show business. She's just jealous,* she told herself.

She checked her watch. It was just past noon and she didn't want to return to the apartment. *So now what?* She had very little money left—less than ten dollars. It was enough for a quick meal, but then she'd be completely broke. She wondered if she could get some spending money from Billy or Heather. *Just enough to tide her over. Everyone needs a little walking around money.*

Her pussy twitched as she thought about how her request might go over. She hated being so dependent on others. She wished she had a small apartment and a nest egg to draw on while she pursued her dream. *She was sure someone would give her a break.*

If I only had a little more time!

Kristy bought a muffin at a shop for a dollar-seventy-five and ate it quickly. She didn't know where else to go or what to do with the rest of the afternoon. Without any firm direction, she headed off toward the famed Hollywood and Vine. *With luck, she'll be discovered before nightfall.*

Billy was home when Kristy buzzed up to the apartment a few hours later. She wished Billy would loan her a key, but figured that was more trust than he wanted to extend to her. He let her in and gave her a big hug. She melted into his arms. Then she felt his hands on the zipper of her black dress and she froze.

"Hey, relax. We had a deal, remember?"

"Oh, right. Sure, Billy."

He unzipped her dress and helped her step out of it. He waved his hands at her and she blushed and unclasped her bra and let her panties slip down her legs onto the rug. She gathered them up and carried them to her small valise and put them away. The dress she draped over the back of a chair so it wouldn't get too wrinkly.

"Come on, turn around so I can see."

"Is Heather here?"

"No, she's gone. It's just you and me."

She turned and hid behind her hands for a few minutes until he told her to drop them. "We have a deal, right? Where else you gonna find a place to live like this for fifty a night?"

Kristy nodded, her eyes on the floor.

"Relax. Tell me about your day. Did you get your resume done?"

"Uh, yeah." She dreaded handing him the bill.

"Well, let me see!"

She found the folder and handed him a sample. He gave a broad smile.

"This looks great! Now this is the kind of thing that a casting director expects, you know? I like the way he changed it around, emphasizing your acting abilities. This should really help."

"Yes, it should."

Her lack of enthusiasm caught his attention. He looked up. "What's wrong?"

"Uh, Tom gave me his bill." She felt as if she might burst into tears. "I didn't know it was so expensive!"

He frowned. "How much was it?"

"T-two hundred."

Billy went still in that dangerous way of his. "That much, huh?" He seemed to suck in his breath and Kristy cringed.

"You know I'll pay you back, Billy!"

He let out his breath slowly and seemed to regain control of himself. "I know you will, sweetheart. At least you've got everything you need now to make it big in this town."

"Uh, I still need my book." She recounted her efforts to get her prints from Freddie's secretary and how rude she had been. "The thing is, there's an open audition tomorrow. Do you think you could call and ask him if he could get my photos done by the morning? It would really help me to maybe get a job. I'd be out of your hair earlier."

Billy cocked his head at her. "Am I giving you the impression that I want you to leave?"

"Well, I appreciate everything you've done, but...well, I really feel like I've overstayed my welcome."

"Nonsense!" He put down his beer and leaned forward. Kristy tried not to shy away as he enveloped her naked body in his arms. She liked Billy, she told herself—she just wasn't sure she liked how their relationship was going. He seemed too focused on her debts than what a nice girl she was.

Why can't he just like me for me? We could square up the debt later, when I landed my first role.

"It's gonna be okay. I like having you around."

Kristy nodded against his chest. He was comforting and strong and she wished she could just be taken care of and not have to worry about where her next meal might come from. Billy wasn't such a bad guy, she told herself.

"But I still need my photos," she told him. "Can you talk to him?"

He sighed and she thought she had gone too far. But he pulled out his cell phone and made a call. "Freddie? Billy. Hey, you know those photos you took of Kristy? Yeah. Look, she's got an audition tomorrow and...Yeah? Oh, I don't know. That's a lot to ask. I know you're busy. No, that won't work. She'll just have to pick them up Thursday."

Thursday! That was two more days away. "Wait a minute," she said.

Billy looked down at her. "Just a minute, Freddie. Yeah?"

"What did he want? If it'll get the photos done earlier, I'd like to hear it."

He frowned. "Well, Freddie thought you were beautiful. He wants you to pose for him."

Her mouth dropped open. "Ohhh. You mean nude."

"Yeah. I told him you wouldn't."

"But if I did, I could get the photos by tomorrow morning?"

Billy held up a finger and returned to the phone. "Hey, Freddie. If she does, what'll ya pay her? Really? And you'll have the photos ready by tomorrow? Oh, tonight? Yeah, that's better. Hang on."

He held the phone against his chest and told Kristy, "Here's the deal: You go over there tonight for some shots, and he'll pay you three hundred, plus he'll give you your photos from earlier."

"Three hundred?" It didn't sound like enough. "For nude shots?"

"Yeah, these will be test shots. You know, to see how you look. Three hundred is standard."

She thought about it and shook her head. "No, I'd want five."

Billy laughed. "No way, Jose," he said into the phone. "She wants five." He laughed again and said, "Oh yeah right. I'll let you know." He hung up.

"You drive a hard bargain."

"Did he agree?"

He shrugged. "No. He won't pay more than three hundred for a first-timer. But, he said he'd give you the photos for your book if you give him a BJ."

"What? No way!" Kristy felt a flush of embarrassment wash over her.

"I told him that. But when you think of it, what's the harm? I mean, it's not like you haven't done it already. You exchange something you're good at for something you need. Right?"

"But I hardly know the guy!"

"You hardly knew Duane, either. That worked out all right."

She shook her head, trying to make sense of it all.

He bent down and took one of her nipples into her mouth. Kristy dared not push him away. His attentions soon had the desired effect—she felt her pussy moisten and she shivered with desire.

"But that's the deal," he said, pulling away. "If I were you, I'd jump on it. It's not like you'd have to fuck the guy. And you certainly are talented in that area! You'd get your photos early and by tomorrow, you'd be out meeting agents and casting directors. If you were smart, you'd let him take some shots too."

Kristy found she wasn't so worried about giving Freddie a blowjob as much as she worried about being talked into posing for pictures. "I don't want to ruin my reputation."

"Lots of starlets pose for pictures. You see them all the time."

"But I don't want to start out that way."

"Suit yourself." Billy's hand went to her bare mound and began to stroke. She let her legs come apart and enjoyed his attentions. For a few minutes, she drifted, her mind and body going off in separate directions. Suddenly, something clicked in her head and she sat up.

"Hey!"

"What?"

"You don't care if I give the photographer a blowjob?"

He laughed. "I care. But you're not exactly my girlfriend, are ya? In a few days, you'll be off and forget all about old Billy. So I'm just trying to help you get street-smart quickly, that's all."

"So he'd really give me my photos if I did that? Like with Duane?"

"That's what he said."

"Well, shit."

"You want me to call him back?"

Kristy felt her heart pound. "Uh…" She turned to him. "That's kinda weird, isn't it? You encouraging me to go off and suck some guy's cock?"

"In this town, no, it's not weird at all. It's what makes the city work."

She bit her lip. "Okay. I really need those photos. Set it up. No posing! One quick BJ and he gives me my prints. Right?"

"Right." He made the call.

An hour later, Kristy found herself in the elevator riding down to the first floor, her nerves sparking anew. Billy had said his driver lived on the first floor and would take her wherever she wanted to go. When she knocked on Ronald's door, she had to take a step back when the massive black man opened it.

"Uh, Ronald?"

"Yeah, baby." He just stood there.

"Uh, Billy said you'd give me a ride?"

He smiled and eyed her up and down. Kristy felt suddenly naked.

"He didn't tell you my deal?"

She frowned. "Deal? No, he didn't." She thought Ronald worked for Billy—so what deal was he talking about?"

"You gotta show me your panties—I love to see a girl's panties."

Kristy's mouth dropped open. "No way! Billy wouldn't make me do that!"

The big man shrugged. "Sure he would. It's a perk, you see. 'Cause a good driver is hard to find."

She didn't know what to do. She wanted to call upstairs and ask Billy but Ronald seemed so sure of himself.

"Come on, it's just for a second. Just pull up your dress for me."

Kristy looked up and down the hallway. It was deserted. "Do I have to?"

"If you want a ride, you do."

Her hands trembled as she reached for the hem of her dress. She pulled it up and showed him her lacy panties for a quick second and let her dress down. He shook his massive head.

"Uh uh. You gotta let me see until I tell you you can stop."

She repeated her actions, feeling the heat rise up into her face. She endured his dark eyes on her panties for a few long seconds before he nodded.

"Hang on, let me get my keys."

He escorted her out to the garage and helped her into a giant black Escalade. On the way, he made small talk that helped relax her a little. He seemed genuinely interested in her career efforts. Not once did Ronald make any snide comments about where she was going or what she was going to do.

All too quickly, they arrived. It was shortly after six and the sun still shone brightly. Ronald had let her out and told her he would wait. She stood on the sidewalk and stared at the doorway of the studio for a long time before going inside.

A bell jangled. Kristy was grateful to see that the bored receptionist had gone home. She didn't want to let anyone see what she was about to do. All for some lousy photos! It was ridiculous.

Freddie came around from the back and smiled when he saw her. "Hi, Kristy! Come on back." Freddie was a small, dark man with piercing brown eyes. He moved with nervous energy and when he had shot her earlier, he had bounced around from side to side, snapping photos from every direction as he barked out instructions.

She followed him into the studio where he had taken the photos. Her nerves started to get the best of her and she felt her knees shake.

"You sure you don't want to pose for me?" he asked with a wheedling tone. "I can make you look like a real movie star."

"Uh, no thanks. I don't want photos of me circulating around unless I approve of them."

"Lots of girls do it. It's a great way to pick up some extra cash. I've been told you could use some money."

"Yeah. Look, do you have my photos ready?"

His head jerked and he nodded. "Uh, yeah. First things first." He pointed at his groin. Kristy groaned inwardly and dropped to her knees. She fumbled for his pants and soon had his undersized soft cock out. She almost laughed at him.

Taking him into her mouth, she teased him and soon felt him get hard. That pleased her. She supposed she had her dad to thank for her talent. She began to bob up and down on his shaft and heard his voice climb up toward his release.

"Oh! Oh yes!"

A watery stream filled her mouth and Kristy gamely swallowed it. She looked up. "That was nice," she said.

"Oh baby, you were great!"

"Can I get my photos now?"

"Sure." He zipped up and rummaged through his filing cabinet and handed over a packet. She opened it and looked through it quickly. The photos were quite good. She smiled. It had most definitely been worth it.

"Thanks."

"Anytime. And if you ever need a quick five hundred…"

She paused. "I thought you said three hundred."

"Well, five if you sign away all rights."

She nodded. "I'll think about it."

"Sure."

She waved to the skinny photographer and marveled at how easy that had gone. It hadn't even seemed like prostitution.

CHAPTER NINE

I got my pics," she crowed to Billy when she came inside.

"Great! Let me see!" He seemed as eager as she did.

Kristy came forward and handed him a sample photo. They were all the same, consisting of one face shot in the center of the eight-by-ten sheet, with smaller photos around displaying her in different outfits and poses.

"These look great! I'm sure you'll have no trouble finding work now!"

"Thanks so much for helping me out! I'll pay you back pretty soon now, I can feel it!"

"Speaking of which, remember our deal?"

Kristy blushed. "Do I have to?"

"Come on, don't wimp out on me now."

She shrugged off her clothes and stood naked in front of the man, feeling awkward and exposed. Of all the demands that had been made on her in the last few days, Kristy found this to be the most embarrassing. She'd almost rather give a man a blowjob with her clothes on than stand naked under his steady gaze.

Billy acted as if everything was normal. "Did Freddie try to get you to pose?"

"Yes, he did. But I don't want to have nude photos of me circulating around. It could ruin my career!"

Billy shrugged. "In this town, that may not be true. Lots of girls get started that way. It's a good way to get some free publicity, you know."

"I don't understand."

"It's like this. An unknown girl comes in and, to make money, poses for some pictures. The money helps her survive in this town and a few years later, say she lands a film role and becomes a rising star. Then the pictures come out and there's a big scandal, right?"

"Yeah—that sounds terrible!"

"No, actually it works in your favor. Suddenly, everyone's talking about you and your name is everywhere. Directors who are seeking actresses for roles that include some nudity often have trouble casting them. They'll know you'd do it. You'll start getting more calls, more roles. Pretty soon, you're a top actress and those photos only enhance your allure."

Kristy frowned. It didn't make sense to her but the way he explained it, it did. It made her head hurt. "I don't know. I think I'll try to survive other ways."

He reached out and touched the bare skin of her shoulder. She shivered. "So far, you're doing just fine. Look at how far you've come!" He bent down and kissed her on the lips. Kristy melted up against him, enjoying this bit of comfort. He had seemed distant lately and she needed this. His arms wrapped around her and she nestled against his chest.

"Did you give Freddie a blowjob?" He suddenly asked and she froze.

"Uh...yeah."

"See? You already are learning how to use your talents to get your way."

"Yeah, I guess."

"You know, I'd really like to feel that sweet mouth on my cock. Will you do that for me?"

"Uh, gee, Billy..." She wasn't in the mood right now, having just given one to Freddie.

His voice took that hard edge. "Oh? You think giving you a safe place to live isn't as valuable as a few pictures?"

She sighed and slipped down to her knees. She gave in to him, but she felt tawdry and abused. His cock was hard and insistent. She took that spear into her mouth and began to pleasure him while her brain went into neutral. When he came in her mouth, she swallowed and felt tears come to her eyes.

"Do...Do I get some money off my debt to you?"

He looked down at her and shook his head. "That's a perk of the landlord, sweetie. Like having you naked. Unless you'd rather find a better deal somewhere else."

"No, no—I was just asking. I want to pay you back, Billy, I really do. I hope to land this gig tomorrow—it's a horror film. But I'm really broke! I need just a few bucks for small expenses!"

Billy pulled her to her feet so he could look into her eyes. "Tell ya what. I've got a way you can earn more than that. And you'd be knocking some more money off your debt."

Fear flooded through her again. "Uh, no, Billy, that's..."

His face hardened. "What? Was it so terrible with Duane?"

"Well, no, Duane was nice, but I don't want to start paying off all your debts to your friends."

"That's who I'm talking about—Duane! Just Duane."

Kristy nodded, feeling a small sense of relief. "Oh! You mean him again?"

"Yeah. He liked you so much, he wanted to see you again."

"But I thought you paid back what you owed...I mean... you know."

"I did! And thanks for that. But now he wants to have you come by his place and he'll pay me—and I'll split it with you!

You'll get some spending money out of it and you get to stay here a while longer."

"S-s-split it with me?"

"Yeah. Fifty-fifty. We'll charge him two hundred, we each get a hundred. Now, could use you a hundred?" He winked. "Of course, you could always give it to me and pay down your debt! But I'm just kiddin'—you keep half, plus whatever tip you get. Just bring me back my half, okay?"

"Uh, I don't know, Billy...I'm not that kind of girl." She felt ridiculous saying it, nude and vulnerable as she was.

"But this is just business, right? You do me a favor, I do you a favor. I didn't have to open up my home to a runaway, now did I? Where would you be now if it wasn't for me?"

Kristy didn't know the answer to that, but could imagine that it wouldn't have been pretty. She'd be homeless, an innocent girl out among all the crazies.

"I really appreciate what you've done for me, but I don't want to start paying off your friends by...you know."

"What? Using your pussy? It's not so bad to say. I mean, it's a gold mine, if you want to use it now and then. That's all I'm sayin'—girls like you have a built-in money-maker! You can get out of debt anytime you want!"

"Can't I just owe you?"

His face took on that harsh edge that always scared her. "Jeez, Kristy, I'm trying to help you here. You owe me, what, five hundred, right? Three hundred from your debt and two hundred for the resume. You got five hundred?"

She shook her head.

"It's just that I'd like to get some of it paid off as quickly as possible. Can you blame me?"

"Well, no, I guess I can't. But I will pay you! I promise!"

He nodded and took her hands in his. "I know you think I'm some kind of bad guy, talkin' about the debt and how you're costing me money and all…"

Kristy nodded. She did feel that way.

"It's just that a couple a years ago, I did the same thing with another girl. Call me a softy, but I loaned her money for this and that and let her stay here and damn, if she didn't take off on me and owe me a bunch of money! I never saw her or the money again! And she promised me too! So you can understand if I'm a bit jaded."

"But I'm not like her!"

"I know. You say that now. But I can't be sure, you know? So I thought, since Duane called me, that it'd be a good thing all around. You'd get some money, I'd get the debt paid down. Win-win, right? Otherwise, I might hafta ask for the money now."

"Well, I don't know…" She could feel herself wavering and Billy sensed it too.

"You liked Duane, didn't ya?"

"Yeah, he was nice." Even now, Kristy could feel the man's hands on her, his cock in her mouth. She remembered how hard it had gotten so quickly after he had come. Her pussy grew damp as if to say, *Come on, Kristy, don't be a party-pooper!*

"Come on, you do a favor for me and let's get this debt down, huh?"

"Jeez, okay, okay!" *Just this one time*, she told herself. *As soon as I get a job, any job, I'm outta here.*

"Good! It's all set up. He wants to see you at eight. Okay? Just go down to see Ronald and he'll drive ya."

"Yeah, okay." Kristy felt committed, although her mind told her she was making a mistake. There was nothing to be done about it now, she thought.

Billy was lovey-dovey after that. He touched her and rubbed her shoulders and told her how beautiful she was. It was flattering and she found herself enjoying his attentions. She thought he might want to make love to her himself and was willing, but he never went further than kissing her breasts.

She made both of them dinner while still nude and found she was starting to get used to it. At the table, she sat across from him, her breasts on proud display and made small talk.

"Heather sure must be working hard. I hardly see her anymore."

"Oh, she's got some modeling deals going on," Billy said vaguely.

Kristy tried to picture Heather in nude photos and couldn't really visualize it. She had no frame of reference for nude photography, other than what she had seen online and that stuff was quite graphic. She couldn't imagine Heather would be doing anything so obscene.

After dinner, Kristy cleaned up and went into the bathroom to get ready for her "date." She was glad she already knew Duane. It made an intolerable situation marginally better. He'd been nice to her.

After showering, Kristy looked over her meager collection of clothes and despaired. What should she wear to this thing? She had worn her black cocktail dress a few times already and it was getting a bit wrinkled. But it was all she had that looked the least little bit dressy, so she put it on.

When she came out, Billy took one look at her and whistled. "You look nice, but..." He paused. "Hang on." He went down the hall to Heather's room and returned a few minutes later with a beautiful silk dress, dark blue in color.

"Wow! I can't wear that! It's Heather's!"

"She won't mind, trust me. I bought it for her. Come on, at least try it on for me." He held it out and she took it. She started to go back into the bathroom and he said, "Whoa. Try it on out here. You know the deal."

"Yeah." She slipped her black dress off and he handed over the blue one. It fit her well, although it was shorter than hers. It came to mid-thigh.

"It's too short! I'll feel exposed if I go out like this!"

"You got panties on, dontcha? You'll be fine. You do look beautiful, you know."

"Really?" She went to the full-length mirror at the end of the hall and turned to look at herself. It was a beautiful dress. "Well, okay."

"Great! It's all set. Now just go on down. Ronald knows where to go."

Kristy nodded. "Okay." She felt her nerves jangling. She was going out to fuck a man she barely knew! It was surreal.

"Come on, don't worry! It'll be fun. Just bring me back my money, okay?" He winked when he said it, but she knew he was serious.

CHAPTER TEN

Night had fallen when Ronald pulled up in front of an apartment building about fifteen minutes away from Billy's place. He leaned over the back seat and told her Duane's apartment number.

"Just call me when you're done," he said handed her a cell phone. "Just hit number three."

Kristy fought her fears and got out. Duane buzzed her in and she waved goodbye to Ronald and he drove off. She found the elevator and rode up to the fifteenth floor. Her nerves seemed to ratchet up a couple notches as she walked down the corridor.

It's just Duane, she told herself. *You've done this before.*

Surprisingly, her pussy was already wet with anticipation. What was that about, she wondered.

She rang the bell and Duane opened it at once. "Hello, little lady!" A big smiled creased his face. She stepped inside and noted that he had a very nice place as well. As her eyes swept over the room, she froze—there were two strange men in the living room.

"Uh, I didn't know you had company," she said nervously. "I can come back later."

"Oh, no, these are just some of my homeboys, stopping to visit. Come on in and I'll introduce you."

He put his hand at her back and practically pushed her into the living room. The two men grinned at her. Both were African-American. One was good-looking like Duane, with muscles rippling under his tight shirt and a smooth complexion. The other was, frankly, a bit scary to look at. He was heavy-set and bald and had pock-marked skin. Kristy smiled at them both with false politeness.

"Gentlemen, this is Kristy. Kristy this is my man Chris," he said, pointing at the good-looking man. He got up and once and gave her a hug.

"Hey, Kristy," he said.

She was taken by surprise but she didn't object.

"Hey, that's funny, isn't it? Kristy and Chris," Duane said.

They all laughed.

"And this motherfucker is Leon," he said. The ugly man didn't get up. He just nodded at her from the couch and made a kissing face. She blushed and wished she were somewhere else. How was this supposed to work? She had expected Duane would be here alone. She felt trapped.

"Come, sit, relax. They don't bite." He looked over at Leon. "Well, we're not too sure about him!"

Everyone laughed except Kristy, who thought it might be true.

Duane sat on an upholstered chair and pulled Kristy down to his lap. Her dress rode up and she fought to cover herself, remembering her robe from the night before. How did she manage to get herself into these situations?

"Now, Kristy here is an as-pir-ing actress," he said, stressing the syllables. He made it sound like a joke.

"Great," Chris said. "We can always use another actress in this town."

He and Leon laughed and high-fived each other, but Kristy didn't get the joke.

"What kind of things do you wanna do?" Leon asked. It was a thoughtful question from the big man.

"Uh, I'm not sure. Just about anything to get started. But later, I'd like to do TV or movie roles."

"I'm sure you'll make it," Duane said, his hands touching her back, making her feel more nervous in front of these men. She didn't want to be here.

"You sure are a pretty girl," Chris said.

"Uh, thanks." She wished they'd leave so she could be alone with Duane. But he seemed oblivious to her nervousness. His hands kept touching her and she had a sudden fear that he would do to her tonight what Billy had done last night—fondle her in front of his friends. She squirmed in his lap and tried to get up. He held her firmly in place and she soon gave up.

"I think our guest could use a glass of something. What you want, honey? We have beer, wine, liquor...?"

"Uh, some wine, I guess." Yes, that might help. She wasn't a big drinker, but she wanted to seem sophisticated among these older men.

"I'll get it," Chris said and jumped up.

"How old are you, honey?" Leon asked.

"Uh, eighteen."

"Wow, you don't look a day over sixteen! Are you sure you're not lying to us?"

"No, no I'm not."

"Youth is valuable in this town," Duane said. "Especially girls who look young but are legal."

Kristy didn't like the way the conversation was going. "I really should—"

"No, no," Duane said. "We have a deal here, don't we?"

She realized she wouldn't be allowed to leave until she had fulfilled her duty. Her mouth went dry.

Chris returned with the wine and handed it to her. He had nearly filled the glass with the amber liquid. She took a big gulp and choked and began coughing. Duane helped her by slapping her on her back until her airway cleared.

"Take it easy, we don't want to lose you this early in the evening," he joked.

"I'm just...I really think..."

Duane finally seemed to sense her growing nervousness. "Hey, baby, come with me." He helped her to her feet and turned back to the two men. "You boys behave yourselves, ya hear?"

They laughed.

He led her down the hall to the bedroom. "Now you just wait in here for me, okay? Drink your drink; it'll help calm your nerves."

Kristy was relieved to be away from those crude men. "Okay. But I, uh, can come back later. I don't want to interfere with your, uh, friends."

"Don't be silly. Those motherfuckers can entertain themselves. Now just hang on. You need some more wine?"

"No, I'm okay."

Duane left and she looked about the bedroom. It had an African theme and seemed to have been professional decorated. Duane must make a lot of money, she thought. *It wouldn't hurt to be nicer to him*, a scolding voice in her head said. The bed appeared to be a king-sized, with an African-patterned bedspread. On the wall were some wooden masks and shields made out of reeds. The lighting was soft but small spotlights illuminated everything on the walls. It looked like something she might see on HGTV.

She heard raucous laughter from the living room and shivered. How was this supposed to work? She would just wait here until Duane could slip away from his guests and come back here for a quick fuck? It didn't make sense.

The door opened and she turned to see Duane come in. He closed the door behind him. "Now, I know this wasn't what you expected."

"You could say that again. I mean, the way it was explained to me, it would just be me and you."

"I know. Those guys showed up unexpectedly. You know how it is."

Kristy didn't, but she didn't argue the point. She took another sip of wine. The alcohol soothed her nerves.

Duane came forward and took the glass from her hands and placed it on top of a dresser. "Now, as I remember, you were a whiz at cock-sucking."

Kristy blushed and felt heat rise in her face. "Well, uh…"

"Don't be shy. It's a good thing." He wrapped her in his arms and she felt like a little girl against his strong chest. "So how 'bout you suck my cock now?"

"Uh, okay," she said. It all sounded a bit rushed. She had expected he might take some time to help her get into the mood.

She eased down to her knees and unzipped his pants. He surprised her by stopping her. She looked up, questioningly. "What's wrong?"

"First rule—get the money first."

"Oh!" She had quite forgotten about being paid. She nodded. Yes, she was supposed to get two hundred and bring a hundred back to Billy. "Okay. Uh, I need two hundred."

"Good girl," he said, reaching for his wallet and pulling out two bills. "Always get the money up front."

He handed it over. Two hundreds, she noted. She slipped them into her purse.

"Okay, now it would help stimulate me if you'd show me your tits."

She looked up at him, mouth ajar. "Uh, well, okay." Her heart pounded. She slipped the straps down and pulled the dress under her bra. She reached around and unfastened the clasp and let her breasts show. The dress slipped down to her waist and threatened to fall off of her entirely.

Duane nodded. "Very nice."

Kristy unzipped him and his cock sprang out. It was a very nice cock, she remembered. Her mouth began to water despite her nervousness. She took him inside and began to fellate him, using all her talents to handle the large spear of flesh.

"Oh, yes, baby, that's good."

She pushed her thinking mind aside as she worked her magic to please him. She expected he'd want to come in her mouth and later fuck her, just like before. With luck, she might be able to get out of here in a half-hour. Her mouth began to move faster.

"God, that's good, baby. Oh yeah. Here it comes!"

Kristy steeled herself and felt his cock squirt into her throat. She swallowed quickly and pulled back, gasping for air.

"Oh! You have a very talented mouth! I'm tellin' you, baby, you could make a fortune with it!" He zipped up.

Kristy stared up at him, confused. Was that it? All he wanted was a blow job? She wasn't sure if she should get up and leave or wait for him to recover. Suddenly, she heard another voice.

"Really? She's that good?"

Her head whipped around to see Chris standing in the doorway. She gasped and pulled her dress up over her breasts and tried to make herself small. She expected Duane would order him to leave, but he just laughed.

"Oh yeah, man, she's a talent! But she's not free!"

Chris came forward. "Oh, I got money. How much for a blowjob, honey?"

Kristy looked up, eyes pleading. "Please..."

"Come on, can't you use some extra money? I thought you wanted to make enough to move out and get your own place, right?"

"But...I don't want to...I don't know him!"

"Don't be silly! You didn't know me before and that didn't stop you!"

He was right, of course. Still, it felt wrong. She shook her head.

Chris came forward and pulled out his wallet. "So what does she charge for a BJ?"

"Well, I got a special deal, everything for two hundred. But for you, I'm thinking, one hundred for a BJ and two more bills for a fuck." He turned to Kristy. "That seem about right?"

She shook her head harder now. "No, I'm not that kind of girl."

Duane laughed heartily. "You aren't? What kind are you then? What was all that last night and just now?"

Kristy's face burned. The man was right. She had already debased herself. What moral high ground did she think she was standing on? Chris thrust two bills into her hands and she looked down to see they were fifties. She fumbled with her purse and slipped them inside.

"Hey," Chris said to Duane. "You're not gonna watch, are ya?"

"No, I'll go. You kids have fun."

Kristy's eyes were filled with tears and she didn't see Duane leave, but she heard the door close. She blinked and looked up to see Chris standing over her, his hand unzipping his pants.

"Now, let me see those nice tits. Help me get in the mood."

She let her dress drop and he whistled when he saw her ample breasts. "Very nice." He pulled his cock out and Kristy was relieved to see it was of average size. Before she could really think about it, she took his cock inside and began to please him.

"Damn, girl, you're good. Where you learn that? Back in high school?" He laughed and Kristy's face burned. Still, she kept at it. The sooner he came, the sooner she could go home.

His cock swelled in her mouth and she reached up and stroked his balls. He gasped and came in her mouth. She pulled back and swallowed and got another blast on her cheek. Chris laughed and said, "Damn, girl, you are one fine cock-sucker!"

She sagged down, glad that her ordeal was over. Unless Duane wanted to fuck her, she realized. He had paid his two hundred...

Chris zipped up and Kristy stared at the rug, wishing he would leave and Duane would come back in to tell her she was done. But when she saw another set of shoes suddenly appear near Chris's, she looked up to see Leon standing there. She began to shake her head violently back and forth and covered up her breasts with her arm.

"No, no, no..."

Leon's face darkened. "Whatssa matter, bitch? I'm too ugly for ya?"

"No, it's not that," she tried to explain.

He ignored her. "Oh, that mouth is fine for Chris and Duane, but ugly Leon wants somethin', then this white girl is too high and mighty!"

"No, please…"

Leon unzipped his pants and a large, semi-erect cock flopped out.

"Hey man, you gotta pay the girl first," Chris said.

"What is it? Fifty bucks?"

"No, a hunnert. She's prime, I'm tellin' ya."

"Shee-it. Hunnert? That's a lot of scratch."

"She won't take less." He turned to Kristy. "Right? You won't take less than a hunnert for a BJ?"

Kristy didn't know what to say. She didn't want to do this at all. They mistook her shaking of her head for an answer and Chris turned to Leon and said, "See? She's got standards, this girl."

"Okay, okay. Shee-it. But she'd better be good, that's all I'm sayin'." He pulled out a hundred and passed it over. Kristy held it in her hand, her mind not comprehending that she had just agreed to perform a sex act with this scary man. Leon turned to Chris. "You don't need to watch, unless you get off on that sort of thing.'"

Chris chuckled. "Hell, no, man. I just wanted to make sure you treated this fine piece of ass right, you know?"

He left and Kristy looked up to see she was alone with Leon.

"Please, Leon…" she began.

"Hey! You took my money, now get busy. And let me see those tits. In fact, take off the dress entirely. I like to have my dick waxed by a nekkid bitch."

"I'm sorry, I don't want to…"

He slapped her suddenly across the face. She gasped and stared up at him. "I'm not foolin' around here, bitch. You take the money, you perform the service, ya dig?"

She looked down to see she still held his money in her hand. She tried to give it back. He slapped her again.

"I'm not fuckin' around here, now!"

Kristy dropped the bill on the rug and took his cock into her mouth. He pulled back immediately. "That's better, bitch, but lose the dress first."

She stood for a second and let her dress slip off her hips and puddle around her feet. She was left dressed in just her panties. She took Leon's cock into her mouth and tried to concentrate on her technique. That was all that mattered. Her mouth knew what to do. Once she got into the rhythm of it, her mind seemed to go elsewhere and in a few minutes, she heard Leon cry out and felt a blast of hot seed in her mouth. She choked and coughed and pulled back.

"See, that wasn't so bad, was it?"

She shook her head but did not look up. Leon zipped up and left her there, a naked, sodden mess. She didn't move for several minutes as she slowly gathered her wits about her. She didn't bother covering herself.

Okay, time to go, she told herself. She grabbed her purse and noticed the hundred lying on the rug. She stuffed it inside and pulled her dress up. She was trying to fasten her bra when Duane walked back into the room. She glared at him accusingly.

"You bastard! I didn't agree to all that!"

He shrugged. "You got paid, didntja?"

She dismissed her ill-gotten gains with a shake of her head. "I'm leaving!"

"No you're not."

Fear shot through her as she stared at him. "What?"

"I paid you two hunnert, remember? I still am owed a fuck."

Her anger flared up now. "No way! I didn't agree to be a sex toy for your friends! You don't get anything else!"

Duane just smiled and took out his cell phone. "Well, let's see what Billy has to say about that, hmm?" He dialed a number as Kristy slumped on the rug, staring, her mouth ajar.

"Hey, Billy! It's Duane." He nodded and smiled down at the girl. "Yeah, I got your girl here. She says she doesn't want to fulfill her side of the bargain..."

Kristy's eyes flashed. "Dammit! I did more than that!"

"Here," he said, thrusting the phone at her. "He wants to talk to you."

Her hands shook as she grabbed the phone. She was going to give Billy a piece of her mind. Before she could speak, she heard him bark at her: "Hey, bitch! Don't embarrass me! I owe Duane a lot and if you know what's good for ya, you'll be nice to him and his friends or I'll toss your ass out on the street tonight!"

"But, Billy..."

"I know you're makin' some good money there and you'll need it to pay me back! If you do what you're told, you can stay with me longer. If you don't, you can pay me what you owe and hit the road, you dig?"

"But I'm scared, Billy!"

His voice softened at once. "I know, baby, I know. But my man Duane there is a sweetheart. If you're nice to him, he'll be nice to you, okay? It's not like you haven't fucked him already."

Kristy felt the skin on her body prickle with shame and embarrassment. "I just want to come home, Billy. Can't I come home? I'll pay you what I've made and we'll be square."

"If you come home now, you'll pay me what you made, yeah, but you'll have to leave at once. You got a place to go? If

I were you, I'd earn some good money, pay me some and have some left over so you can find yourself an acting job."

Kristy knew she was trapped. She didn't want to be kicked out, not in the middle of the night. "Okay," she said in a small voice. "But I'm scared."

"Let me talk to Duane."

She handed the phone over.

"Yeah? Oh, of course. All right. I'll take good care of her. Yeah, okay, she does seem to be a little scared. All right. Sorry, man." He hung up.

Duane bent down so his eyes were on her level. "I'm sorry you got so scared. Get dressed and come on out and sit with us and have some wine. We'll all be nice, okay? We know this is all new for ya."

He found a tissue and helped Kristy clean up her face.

Kristy nodded, grateful for the small measure of kindness. But what she really wanted was to be allowed to leave. She rose and pulled her clothes together and followed Duane out into the living room. The two men gave her big smiles when they saw her, but their smiles faltered when Duane ripped into them.

"Hey, you assholes! You scared the girl here. "She's all messed up and thinks we're a bunch of animals." Now I want to show her we can be nice, all right?"

Chris and Leon both bobbed their heads in contrition.

"Hey, we're sorry, dollface. We thought you liked us," Chris said.

"I know I'm ugly, maybe it was my fault," Leon said. "I didn't know black guys scared you."

They both seemed so genuinely ashamed that Kristy felt a pang of guilt. Was she just being racist?

"No, it's okay," she said at once. "I'm all right. I was just scared for a bit. It happened so fast."

"Where's this girl's wineglass?" Chris said. "You're not being such a good host yourself, you know, man."

Duane nodded. "You're right. We left it in the bedroom. I'll get it."

She sat down across from the couch and licked her lips. It was very strange, sitting here trying to be nice to two men who had minutes ago had practically forced themselves on her. But her social training kicked in and she tried to make them understand she wasn't a racist.

"It's not that you guys are black," she said. "It's just all so sudden, you know?"

"Sure, baby, I know. I'm sorry if I scared you. I want you to like us," Chris said.

"I'm not...that kind of girl. I mean, usually. I'm here to be an actress...that's all."

"I think you'd make a fine actress," Leon said. "Did you know that I was in a movie once?"

"Really?"

"Yeah, I was a bad guy in 'Desperate Measures.' You ever see it?"

Kristy shook her head. "No, I didn't. I'm sorry."

Chris laughed. "Oh, it was a straight-to-DVD flick. Critics gave it one star."

"Hey, at least I was in somethin'!" Leon retorted, but with good-natured humor.

She began to relax. They weren't such bad guys, she told herself. They just got a little frisky. Now that they've all come, they were actually pretty nice.

Duane came back with her wine glass and stopped in the kitchen to top it off. He handed it over and she took a big sip.

For several minutes, the three men and the small girl sat around talking and drinking. Kristy began to relax after her second glass of wine and found herself laughing at some of the men's jokes.

Finally, Duane looked at his watch. "Well, it's getting late. Come on, Kristy, let's take care of some business, then I'll take you home."

Kristy glanced up, not sure what he meant at first. But his expression told her everything.

"Uh…"

"Come on, I've got my second wind." He winked at the other men.

She looked over and saw that same hungry look.

"Can't we wait…?"

"You heard Billy. We had a deal, he and I. Come on, I won't hurt ya."

Reluctantly, she stood up, feeling a bit tipsy. She cast a fearful glance at the two men, wondering if they would stay out here, listening to them in the bedroom? Or would they go?

"You guys stay here and behave yourselves," Duane said, winking. So much for them leaving, she thought.

She followed Duane back to the bedroom. Once inside, he motioned to her dress and she allowed it to slip free. He nodded and she unclasped her bra and stepped out of her panties. As she stood naked in front of him, she was reminded of how often she'd been naked in front of Billy lately, so she should be used to this. Still, she felt her nervousness returning.

He came forward and enveloped her into his arms. It made her feel better and she relaxed, feeling her nipples press against his shirt. He bent down and picked her up and she felt tiny in his arms. He laid her on the bed and stepped back. His clothes came off quickly and Kristy remembered how muscular he was. It sent a shiver through her.

Duane was gentle, which helped ease any fears she may

have had. He kissed her all over and she grew wet and her desire rose. When he reached for a condom, she was ready for him. Her fears had largely vanished. She had been so silly, she scolded herself. Duane really was a nice guy.

He entered her slowly and she welcomed him. His stroking was smooth and gave her great pleasure. He was being a very generous lover, making sure she climaxed before he did. It allowed her to let go and climb toward her orgasm.

"Oh! Oh yes!"

She lost her inhibitions as first one, then a second orgasm rocked her. Seconds later, she felt his cock throb deep within her and she cried out and hugged him close. At last, they pulled apart.

"That was nice," he said. "Thank you."

She felt bad that she had treated him poorly. "No, thank you. I'm sorry I was such a baby."

"It was just too fast. I understand."

She nodded.

Duane got up, tossed the condom and pulled on his pants. She started to rise as well, but he held up a hand. "No, no, you just relax."

Kristy sank back down against the sheets. She wanted to go, yes, but it felt good to relax and come down from her high. He opened the door and immediately, she spotted Chris in the doorway. He came forward as she gasped and pulled the sheet up around her body.

"Hey!" She looked around, but Duane had gone.

He sat on the edge of the bed. "Relax, honey. I just want to talk."

"Talk?"

"Yeah. I want to ask you somethin'—you wanna go home?"

She nodded. "Yes, of course!"

"I thought so." He pulled out his wallet and took out two hundreds. "You fuck me and then you can go home."

Kristy stared at him. Her fears came back and she shook her head. "I don't want to. I want to go home."

Chris frowned. "Come on, you fucked Duane. What's he got that I don't got?"

"It's not that…" She tried to make him understand. "That was a special deal. I had to if I was going to stay in Billy's apartment."

"I think the same deal applies for me, too, you know?"

Kristy realized she was trapped—again. Her mind tried to tell her just to go along, that Chris was nice. But that other part wasn't yet convinced. "I'm not a hooker," she said. "I'm an actress—or at least, I'm trying to be."

"I know you are, honey. But you need money to make it in this town. We're just tryin' to help you out. You dig?"

She nodded. "Yeah, I guess."

"And I'm not a bad guy, am I?"

"No, no, you seem nice." He actually scared her, but she didn't want to admit it.

"Okay then," he said and leaned in to kiss her cheek. She felt his hand on her breast underneath the sheet. "I'm sure a couple hundred would pay for a lot of acting classes, right?"

That was something Kristy hadn't had time to think about. Acting classes would be very good to have, she thought, not even aware how she was rationalizing her situation. She'd already fucked Duane. What's one more guy?

"Okay," she breathed.

He pulled the sheet from her hands and bent down to kiss a nipple. Kristy shivered, and held the back of his head. God, it felt good, despite her fears. It didn't take very long before she found herself in bed with a very naked and strong man, rubbing his hard cock over her sensitive mound.

When he slipped it inside, she gasped, "Condom!"

"Don't worry, baby, I won't come inside." He rammed his cock deep within her and Kristy could only pant in shock. Chris, she quickly learned, was a very energetic lover. He didn't make love—he pounded at her. Her orgasms rose up and crashed over her only to be replaced by another. She forgot all about his bare cock inside and just hung on, gasping and crying and shouting.

Suddenly, she felt his cock swell within her and he yanked it out and came all over her stomach. She cried out in relief and hugged him close, feeling his seed smear over her stomach.

"Oh, baby, you are such a fine piece of ass," he murmured. Kristy was too exhausted to respond.

He got up and began dressing. Kristy lay limply on the bed, not caring that she was exposed.

"Thanks doll, you're a sweetheart," he said and she blushed.

Chris wasn't even out the door when Leon's big frame filled it. Her mouth dropped open. Before she could speak, he tossed two hundred on the bed and jumped on her.

"Hey!" She struggled to wiggle out from underneath his bulk.

He ignored her. She felt him fumble for his pants and unzip himself.

"Hey! Stop! Duane!"

He was too strong for her. In seconds, she felt his huge cock stretch her. "Wait! You have to wear a condom!"

"If I do, will you be nice to ol' Leon?" He said, the head of his cock already forcing its way into her.

"Yes, yes!" she said, willing to do anything to avoid getting pregnant.

He pulled out and sat up. She caught her breath and watched him as he fished a condom out of the nightstand and slipped it on. "That's all I ask, you know," he said. "Is for a girl to be nice to me. I know I'm ugly."

Kristy, despite her fear and embarrassment, couldn't help but be touched by the big man. "No, you're not ugly," she assured him. "You're just a big guy, that's all."

He smiled. "Some girls like a big cock. You like a big cock, white girl?"

"I don't know—I haven't had one before."

Leon guffawed. "Ha! So I'm bigger than all those others guys, huh? I knew it." He eased his bulk over her, but this time, he propped himself up by his elbows to keep from crushing Kristy. She was grateful for this little bit of kindness.

When he slipped the head in, she felt as if her body was being stretched in two. "Wait," she gasped. "Go slow!"

"Aw, you can take it—I hear you farm girls have big pussies."

"Ow! Wait! Uunff!" Her pussy seemed stretched to its limit and still he had more to go. "Wait! Go slow!"

"Okay, baby. As long as you're being nice." He pulled back, allowing her lubrication to coat his massive shaft, easing the passage when he pushed forward again. Bit by bit, Kristy felt the invader press deeper inside her. He eased it in, so it gave her pussy time to adjust. She had never felt anything like it before. When he was fully inside her, he began tiny movements, back and forth. It hurt for a few seconds and then the warmth began to spread. He began to move in and out more completely until his huge cock was ramming her hot pussy, sending shockwaves up to her brain.

"Oh! Oh! Oh god!"

"That's it, baby. You're diggin' it now. All the whores love Leon's cock."

Part of her wanted to tell him she wasn't a whore, she was just an actress, but couldn't convince herself of that lie. Here she was, lying underneath her third man of the evening, fucking his brains out, money scattered around her on the bed.

But she couldn't think about that—she couldn't think about anything at the moment. Leon was rutting with her, his thick cock sliding out and slamming back home. With each thrust, she rode up toward the head of the bed until she had to brace herself with her arms to keep from being knocked out by the headboard.

Leon bellowed and she grunted in response, glad it was over. She hadn't come, but she had faked it enough to please him, apparently.

"How 'bout that, bitch!" He said, slapping her hip and leaving a red mark. "You know you got fucked now!"

"Uh, yeah. It was great," she said.

He got up, tossed off his condom and slipped on his clothes. He found a twenty and tossed it to her. "That deserves a tip, baby. You were great."

"Uh, thanks."

After he left, Kristy just lay there, stunned. She wasn't sure what had just happened. That she had fucked three men was obvious, but what wasn't clear was, had she just helped out Billy or had she just become a whore? She looked around and began gathering up the money. Kristy pulled out the money from her purse and counted it all.

Eight hundred twenty dollars.

"Fuck," she said. It was a hell of a lot of money.

Duane walked in while she was counting it.

"How'd ya do, baby?"

She looked up, not sure if she should admit she had so much. Then she felt a twinge of guilt because that was a racist thought—like he might steal it? "About eight hundred," she said.

"Damn! That's good. That's a fine night's work. Billy will be pleased."

She frowned. She only owed Billy a hundred, she thought. He said he'd split the cost of fucking Duane—these other guys were all on her, right?

"Sure," she said, not willing to admit the private deal she had with Billy.

"Well, you'd better call Ronald. The party's over."

She nodded and dug the cell phone out of her purse. She heard Ronald's voice and he promised to come pick her up in fifteen minutes. She got up and noticed how shaky her legs were. Her pussy throbbed with overuse and her nipples seemed raw.

CHAPTER ELEVEN

Kristy got dressed slowly. When she felt decent, she went down the hall to see Duane talking to the two men near the front door.

"There you are, you sweet bitch," Leon said and enveloped her in his massive arms. She felt his hands all over her ass and tried to smile her way through it. When she felt his hands pull up her skirt and tug at her panties, she jerked and tried to get free. Leon just laughed and yanked her panties down to her knees and ripped them off of her.

"I always get a trophy from a new whore," he said.

She colored and looked to the other men for help, but they just stood there.

Chris was next and he hugged her and she felt his cock harden against her. God, these men were incorrigible! "You promise to see me again, baby?" he asked, grinding himself against her.

"Uh, sure," she promised, saying anything to get away.

She managed to free herself from Chris and then Duane hugged her. He grabbed her breast and squeezed until she squealed. Everyone laughed.

"Well, you'd better get your ass downstairs afore Ronald gets mad," Duane told her. She was happy to escape and heard them all laugh as she ran for the elevator. She had hoped to ride alone, but both men followed her and climbed in when the doors opened.

Kristy felt she had made a mistake but didn't have the courage to ask if she could ride alone, so she just bit her lip and punched the button for the lobby. As soon as the doors closed, Leon grabbed her from behind and began running his hands over her body, pulling up her dress to expose her bare pussy to Chris's leering gaze.

"You like Leon, baby?" he asked.

"Wait, please, stop, my dress!" Kristy said, trying to pull his hands away from her body.

"Ohh, you know you like it, dontcha bitch?" Leon said.

Her dress was pulled up to her stomach and Leon's hand was busy between her legs, trying to arouse her. But Kristy had had quite enough sex that evening and his fingers hurt.

"Please! Stop! It hurts!"

The door dinged and opened suddenly. Kristy looked up to see a middle-aged couple standing there, their eyes open wide. She wanted to ask for help but the sudden look of disgust on the woman's face stilled her tongue.

"My word!" the woman said, staring at her naked pussy being fondled by Leon.

The doors closed and both men laughed.

The elevator started down again and Chris reached out and hit the Emergency button and the car lurched to a stop. Alarm bells went off. He turned to Kristy.

"How 'bout a quickie, since we paid you so good?"

She tried to shrink back, but Leon prevented her from moving.

"Yeah, baby. I could use another blowjob."

"Please, I did what you asked earlier. Let me go!"

"Hold her still, Leon," Chris said and stepped up close, his hand unzipping his pants. Kristy was smashed between the two men and she felt Chris's hard cock slip inside of her.

There was nothing she could do about it—Leon held her up so Chris could fuck her. It didn't take long—in a few seconds, she felt him squirt inside of her and she moaned in frustration and fear.

When he stepped back, she was pushed to her knees and she felt her dress being pulled straight up over her head. She opened her eyes to see Leon's cock jutting out from his pants and heard him snarl, "Get busy, bitch. Ronald's waiting."

There was nothing she could do but obey. She sucked on the man's huge cock, trying to make him come quickly. In the background, she heard Chris hit the button and the elevator began to move. Before she finished, she felt the elevator stop and heard another gasp from someone in the hallway.

She imagined how she must've looked—a naked woman except for her bra kneeling on the floor of an elevator sucking on a big man's cock. Anyone would think she was a slut! The doors closed again and she worked harder in order to satisfy him and was rewarded with a shout and a dribble of come in her mouth. She sagged back in relief.

"Good girl," Leon said and handed her the dress.

Kristy slipped it on just as the car reached the lobby and nearly ran toward the door, the laugher of the two men echoing in her ears. Ronald was waiting outside in the Escalade and she jumped into the back.

"How did it go?" he inquired, as if she had just come from a PTA meeting.

"Uh, fine. Let's just go!" She watched as Leon and Chris came out and waved at her. She watched Ronald wave back before he pulled out.

Kristy sank into the back seat and tried to keep from crying.

When she returned to Billy's apartment, her ordeal wasn't over, she was quick to learn. Billy was waiting up for her.

"Hey, dollface, how did it go?"

"Oh, Billy, it was awful! Duane wasn't alone! He had two friends over. They...took turns! They practically raped me!"

"Really? Weren't you nice to Duane, like I asked?"

"Yes! I was nice! I thought it would just be Duane! They... they were...They forced themselves on me! It was too much!" Hot tears came to her eyes. "I could be pregnant!" She told him about the unprotected sex in the elevator.

"Oh, we'll take care of that. I'll get you on the pill right away. I know a doctor." He paused. "I hope they all paid you," he said, his voice coldly calm.

Kristy looked up, shocked. "Well, yes—but I didn't want to...do it! Don't I have a say?"

"Not if you got paying customers, sweetie. I mean, you made a lot of money tonight, right? And you needed money, right? It's no different than if a director asked you to pretend to be a hooker for a film."

Kristy could see a lot of difference but before she could launch into her argument, Billy startled her by asking, "So how much did you make, anyway?"

"Uh..." She tried to stall. She didn't want him to know. She wanted to keep it all to herself. After all, she had earned it!

Billy just grabbed her purse and said, "You always gotta tell me, babe. That's the rules."

"Wait! That's my money!"

"No it isn't. I made it happen, didn't I? Besides, you owe me a lot of money. Let's get that square right now."

He pulled out the wad of money and counted it. He whistled. "Shit! Eight hundred! Wow." He tossed her one-hundred and the extra twenty. "You can keep that."

"What!?? I earned all that! That's mine!"

Billy counted out the bills again and stuffed them into his pocket. "Not if you want to live here, it's not. You like this place?"

She shook her head. "I want to get my own place! That's what the money's for! To pay you back and get my own apartment!"

"You owed me five-fifty, including tonight's rent, so I took that off the top. One-twenty to you. That leaves one-fifty. Consider it future rent. That'll keep you safe here for another three days. So it's a good deal all around, right?"

"No! That's mine!" She had worked so hard for it. How could he just keep it? "I have expenses too! I need new clothes, acting lessons! Please, Billy!"

"Why didn't you say so! Tell ya what. Tomorrow, you and I will go downtown and see a doctor and buy some nice shit, all right?"

"But...but..."

"Come on, baby, I'll buy you what you need. All you have to do is ask."

Kristy felt burned and she wanted to talk to Heather about this. Maybe she could help her. She might be able to talk some sense into Billy. She wanted to walk off in a huff but she had nowhere to go. Instead, she went into the kitchen and found a beer and took a big gulp. That calmed her down a bit and she came back to stare angrily at Billy.

"Hey, remember our deal—you gotta be naked."

"Fuck you!" She shouted.

He got up at once and approached her. Kristy tried to look defiant. Suddenly, his hand lashed out and caught her flush on the cheek. She squealed and dropped to the carpet, her beer falling from her hand and spilling. She cowered there, her face burning.

He bent down and picked up the beer before he offered to help her up. She shrugged off his hand and sat up. Her head buzzed.

"Now I can be nice, but I won't tolerate that kind of disrespect," he said, his voice soft, which made it more menacing. "So you be nice."

Kristy nodded and touched her cheek. She could feel it swelling already. She was more determined than ever to leave, but how? How could she get away from this man without money?

"Now, have you decided to be nice and obey the rules?"

Her hands shook as she peeled off her clothes. When she was naked, he made her give him another blowjob, although he didn't come this time. Kristy suspected he just wanted to humiliate her—and it worked.

Fortunately, it was getting late and Billy left her after another half-hour and went off to bed. Kristy climbed onto the couch and hugged the blanket to her, trying to figure a way out of her predicament.

She was awake, having only dozed fitfully, when she heard Heather come in. She got up and once and threw on her robe and went to greet her only friend.

"Heather!" she whispered.

Heather looked exhausted and seemed surprised to see Kristy up so late.

"Hi. What are you doing up? It's late!"

"I know. But I had to talk to you!"

Heather nodded. "Okay. Let me get a drink." She went to the kitchen and found a beer and returned to sit on the couch with Kristy. In the light from the kitchen, she could see

Heather's makeup was smeared and her clothes rumpled. She could also faintly smell the scent of sex on her friend.

But that didn't make sense, she told herself. Heather was on a photo shoot...Suddenly, her mouth dropped open. "Oh my god."

"What?"

"These photo shoots you've been on—you've been fucking guys too, haven't you?"

Heather took a big swig of beer and gave Kristy a steady look. "Yeah. I mean, a girl's gotta survive, right?"

It all made sense now to Kristy. She cursed herself for being so naïve. She had fallen in with a prostitution ring. "So you're a...a..."

"Whore?"

Kristy nodded.

Heather shrugged. "Yeah."

"But...why? Why stay?"

"I could ask you the same thing. I mean, it's not so bad, really. Billy gives me a nice place to stay and buys me whatever I need."

"Not so bad? He makes you whore yourself out for him?" She remembered how casually he had taken nearly all of her money.

"Yeah. But as pimps go, he's better than others."

"Why don't you leave? Go find another job or go to the cops?"

She laughed. "Oh right—if I went to the cops, I'd be putting myself behind bars. If I left, where would I go? The streets? You know how it is out there."

"But with the money you're making, you should be able to keep some for yourself! Why does Billy get so much of it?"

"That's the way it works. I make money for Billy, he takes care of me. He'll take good care of you, too. Nobody fucks with Billy's girls."

Kristy was appalled. "I didn't agree to this! I'm leaving!"

"Sure," Heather said. "You can go anytime. But you'll be right back out there, trying to survive. You know how many girls try to live on the streets here? Hundreds. And every day, one or two wind up dead from a beating, a knifing or a drug overdose. You think you got it bad here? You ain't seen nothin' until you live like a rat out there." Heather turned away and blinked back tears.

"You sound as if you've tried it yourself."

Heather nodded. "I was like you once. Full of plans to be an actress. And when Billy snapped me up, I thought it was a good deal too, at first. When I found out what he wanted from me, I took off. I had no money but I didn't care. I was going to be an actress, not a hooker. So I left and scrounged around for meals and a place to crash..." She bit her lip and Kristy reached out and touched her arm in compassion.

"Two weeks after I left, you know what I was doin' to survive? Yeah, that's right. I was selling blowjobs for enough money to buy food and sleeping in an abandoned warehouse with a bunch of other kids. One night, I ran into a guy who decided he didn't want to pay me."

She stood suddenly and Kristy could only stare as Heather pulled her dress off over her head. She pointed to a puckered scar that ran from her left ribcage to her navel. Kristy gasped.

"He cut me good. I nearly died before they got me to the hospital. You know who I saw when I woke up? Billy." More tears flowed and she didn't bother to brush them away. "He paid for all my medical expenses and he brought me home with him to recuperate. And when I was healthy again, he told me he'd put me to work in a safe way so I'd never have to worry about getting hurt again."

"And you accepted?"

"Of course I did! What choice did I have! I woulda died if it hadn't been for Billy. I only hope you realize that before you do something foolish." She stroked her scar and added, "You think I could get hired as an actress now, with this?" She laughed derisively. "Maybe in a horror pic—but not for any love scenes!"

Kristy didn't know what to say. She stared at Heather and realized just how easy it was to become trapped in Billy's world. It all became clear—everything had been planned: the sudden visit from Duane and being made to fuck him, the sucking off the photographer to get her photos, the two friends of Duane's who had just happened to show up when she was expected. She had been set up.

She found herself shaking her head. "I'm not going to stand for this. I gotta get outta here."

"And go where?" Heather scoffed. "Don't make the same mistake I did. You may not survive."

"They can't allow that sort of thing to happen in this town, can they? What about city leaders, the police? Don't they have programs for this sort of thing?"

"They do, but they're all overwhelmed. Girls flood this town every day, just like you. They pour into the bus stations or airports with a suitcase and a dream. Few make it."

"But I didn't come to Hollywood to be a whore!"

"I know you didn't, honey. Neither did I. But I'm glad to be alive and have a nice place to live and regular meals. I hope to God you listen to me and don't try to run off and make it on your own. You could wind up dead. I've seen it happen too many times."

Kristy tried to think of a response, but nothing came to mind. She was an idiot, a naïve little fool. She had mistaken Heather's and Billy's friendship as genuine. But they both had a hidden agenda. How could she have been so stupid?

"I have to get out of here."

"Please! Think about it first. That's all I'm asking. Think about it."

Kristy could only nod. She felt torn in two. Part of her said she should flee at once, get away from this horrible pimp. But her fear of the city was equally as strong, especially after hearing Heather's story.

"I've got an audition tomorrow, so I'll go to that and decide later, okay?"

"Good. That's all I'm asking—just don't do anything rash. You could do a hell of a lot worse than Billy, I'm telling you."

Heather went off to bed, leaving Kristy alone to think. It was too much to process. She decided to see how the open audition went and take it from there. That made sense.

CHAPTER TWELVE

Kristy stood in the hot sun for hours with other hopefuls, both men and women. With her new hairdo, resume and photos, she felt like one of them for the first time since she had arrived. She clutched them proudly, glad that she had gotten them in time, even if she did have to pleasure Freddie. It would be worth it if she got the job.

The line moved slowly. She wished she had gotten here earlier, but Billy took her to his doctor first thing in the morning to get a "morning after" pill and birth control pills.

"Just as a precaution," he told her. "Normally you make the guys wear condoms."

By the time she got to the audition, the line had snaked around the block. Having nothing else to do—and convinced that once they took one look at her they'd have to have her—Kristy elected to wait.

Shortly before one o'clock, just when she was in sight of the door to the theater where the auditions were being held, a man came out carrying a clipboard. He waved his arms.

"May I have your attention, please?"

The crowd grew quiet. Behind her, Kristy heard someone groan.

"Thank you all for coming, but the cast has been filled! We have all the actors we need!"

The groans increased in volume and people began moving away. Kristy just stood there, stupefied. All her efforts had been for naught. She was no closer to a job than she was before and all the fancy headshots and resumes in the world wouldn't help her.

With a heavy heart, she moved on down the sidewalk, feeling sweaty and bedraggled. Tears came to her eyes and she didn't bother brushing them away. Twin tracks coursed down her cheeks and she cursed herself, her life and Billy. Even Heather drew some of her anger and frustration.

Her only salvation, she told herself, was she had a nice place to stay. For a few more days, at least. But what would Billy demand of her next?

When she got to the apartment and rang, no one answered. She slumped down outside the door in the meager shade and cursed her luck. *I should at least have a key!* she thought. She was glad she had some money. It was lunch time and she decided to splurge and sit in an air-conditioned restaurant.

She found a diner two blocks down the street and went in. She sat at the counter, her book by her side, and ordered a big glass of iced tea. She drank it all at once and got a refill and drank half of that before she ordered.

When she went to pay her bill after lunch, Kristy had to admit it felt good to have a few dollars to spend. And Billy had promised her he'd take her shopping. She could certainly use some new clothes. But at what cost? That was her dilemma. She wondered if she could survive just long enough to land an acting job. Then she could be free of Billy. No one would have to know what she did to survive. And the men had been nice, so far. Duane and the others. Even Freddie had seemed harmless.

She returned to the apartment and this time, Billy was home. He buzzed her up and when she entered the apartment, she found her fingers were automatically reaching for her dress.

She paused and looked around. There didn't seem to be anyone home except Billy. He stared at her and said nothing.

Kristy quickly stripped, feeling like a sex object—which is exactly what Billy wanted her to feel like. He smiled when she was naked and came forward to give her a long kiss, his hands roaming over her body.

"How did it go?"

"Like shit. They filled all the roles before I even got to the head of the line."

"Hmm. We'll get you there earlier next time."

"I know, but it's so frustrating! I never knew how many actors there were in this town."

"But you've got something special—you've got that fresh farm look. Just keep at it, baby."

"Yeah."

She heard a noise and turned to see Heather coming out from her bedroom. Kristy felt exposed and embarrassed and went at once to the couch to sit down. Billy laughed.

"Hey, don't get shy on me all of a sudden! Heather's already seen ya!"

Heather nodded. "Sure. It's no big deal, Kristy." She didn't seem to pay any attention to Kristy's nudity. She went into the kitchen and poured herself some orange juice.

"Ronald says you had a pretty good night."

Kristy's ears perked up.

"Yeah. It was okay."

"Maybe you could show Kristy the ropes, huh?"

Kristy felt the heat rise in her face and she started shaking her head.

"You think she's ready?"

"I dunno. You ready to make some real money, Kristy?"

"No! Besides, from what I see, I won't get any—you'll just take it all."

"Hey, I take care of my girls! Didn't I say I'd buy you some clothes and shit?"

"Yeah, you *say* that..."

Billy nodded at Heather. "When she's right, she's right. Come on, let's all go shopping."

"Really?" Heather said. "I love to go shopping!"

"Yeah, throw on some clothes, Kristy and we'll all go."

Getting dressed sounded really good to her, so she quickly put on a skirt and a blouse from her bag and followed the two down to the garage. Billy had a sleek black BMW and Heather slipped into the passenger seat and Kristy piled into the back. On their way to the mall, they chatted like old friends. For a little while, Kristy was able to forget her troubles. She had to admit, Billy was generous with his money. Although he only bought Heather a couple items, he spent nearly a thousand dollars on Kristy, buying her skirts, tops, sexy new bras and panties—everything she might need to get started in Hollywood.

It was true that everything Billy bought for her had been a little more sexy than she would've bought for herself. But he had talked her into it every time by telling her how good she looked. Whenever she balked, he'd whisper in her ear, "You could wear this around the house instead of goin' nekkid."

When they came home two hours later, Kristy had bags full of mini-skirts, tank tops, lacy bras, thongs and other items. It wasn't until she pulled them out one at a time while she was modeling her purchases for Billy and Heather that she realized she had all the right outfits to be a hooker. She had to change clothes right in front of both of them and it made her feel exposed. But the outfits were very sexy and she had to admit, she did look good in them. She pretended she was in a role of a prostitute with a heart of gold and that made it easier to parade about for Billy.

Over the next couple of days, Kristy went out to find work. She looked up modeling agencies, independent film companies—anything that might give her the break she needed. Every afternoon when she returned home, she felt helpless and hopeless. She was never going to find a job in this town!

When she complained to Billy about it, he just shrugged and said, "I've offered you many ways to make money." They were sitting on the couch. Heather was out for the night. Kristy had on one of her new sexy outfits, but the way Billy was fondling her, she might as well have been naked.

"I'm not going to become a hooker!" she barked and drew away from him.

"Honey, you're already a hooker. You fucked Duane and his friends and you gave Freddie a blowjob in exchange for your photos—don't tell me what you are or are not."

"I'm not going to work for you."

"Oh? So you might work for yourself?"

"It'd be better than giving you my hard-earned money!"

Billy nodded. "Speaking of which, this is your last night here—unless you can start coming up with fifty bucks every day. I'm outta the hotel business."

She stared at him, her face hot. "You're kicking me out? After all I've done for you?"

He shrugged. "It's business, baby. You don't want to work for me, fine. Go find someplace else to live." He slid closer and his hands once again roamed her body. This time, she didn't stop him, thinking if she allowed him free reign, he might change his mind.

Kristy wondered if she might go into business for herself—just temporarily, of course. Just until a job came through. How would that work? She didn't know the first thing about the business end of prostitution. Or how to stay safe in the rough and tumble environment of Hollywood. The truth was, she didn't know what to do and she was afraid to leave this cushy apartment, even if Billy did make certain demands on her. But walking around naked is one thing, fucking strangers was something else entirely.

"You could pose for some pictures if you don't want to hook," he said. His hands moved down and she found herself spreading her legs for him. His fingers moved under her short skirt and began rubbing her clit through her lacy panties.

Kristy shook her head. Having photos out there circulating could ruin her career, despite Billy's assurances that it was considered no big deal in this town. No, she thought, at least hooking doesn't leave any record of her sins.

Billy seemed to sense she was wavering. "Hey, I'm not talkin' about putting you on the streets or anything—I'm just talking about some special deals, like with Duane. You know, guys like him. You go to their place or a nice hotel room, take care of business and come home. You get a place to stay—heck, I'll even give you Heather's room."

That caught her attention. "Heather's room? But...where would she live?"

"I got another place she can crash. Girls are only here temporarily anyway, you see. It was just Heather's turn. She expects she'll be replaced one day soon."

"I couldn't do that to her," she said, but her mind was racing. To have her own room! And it was such a nice apartment! She could really use a steady base of operations—it would give her the breathing room she needed!

"You wouldn't be doing it. I would. Besides, if it isn't gonna be you, it'll be some other startlet, fresh off the bus. You could do a lot worse." His hands felt good. She found herself responding. She was a very sexual person, she told herself. Why not get a little loving and some cash at the same time? No one would have to know. She could go on a few dates and when she got a job, she'd be out of here.

"T-tell me about how it would work. You know..."

"Sure, baby. I gotta lotta friends, you see. Some come from out of town, others are big shots here, you know, like producers and shit..."

"Producers?" Could one of them find her a job? It would be a great way of meeting powerful men who could help her, she thought.

"Sure. Producers, directors, businessmen—you name it." His fingers had slipped under the material of her panties and were stroking her pussy now Kristy was having trouble concentrating. His other hand pulled down her bra and rubbed her nipples and she began to jerk her hips, an orgasm slipping up on her.

"Tell ya what. I gotta guy coming in from out of town tonight. I told him I'd find him a nice girl, you know, not one of those cheap hooker types, but a real class act. You could be that girl. You go see him, take his money, be nice to him, and come home. Easy as pie. I'll give you a key to the apartment and move your stuff into Heather's room. You try it out for a while, okay?"

Her mouth sagged open and she climbed higher toward her release. Fucking someone sounded really good about now. She wished Billy would fuck her. She reached out and grabbed at his pants and started to unbuckle them but his free hand stopped her. Kristy looked up in confusion.

"You gotta make up your mind. You wanna try it out, just to see how it goes?"

Will you fuck me if I do? she wanted to ask, but didn't because she was afraid he'd say no. She didn't want to be rejected. Of course, if she wanted to get fucked, well…

"Okay," she said. "I'll try it, just this one time."

"Good girl." His hand came away from her pussy, leaving her desperate to come. She brought her own hand to finish herself off and Billy grabbed it. "Uh uh. Why don't you save yourself for Charlie? Think of how much better things will go tonight if you're really horny?"

Kristy stared at him. Coming now wouldn't make any difference, but she didn't want to challenge Billy. "Okay," she said softly.

"Good. Let's have some dinner. I'll make some calls and set it up."

Kristy went into the kitchen and started cooking. She felt guilty about Heather, but not so much so that she wanted to tell Billy to forget it. Besides, Heather had another place to live. Billy said he'd see to that. And Kristy promised herself she'd only be here a few more days anyway. She'd keep some of the money she earned and start looking for a cheap apartment. If she played this right, she could turn the tables on Billy—win a juicy role and march out with her head held high. It's not as if she was the only starlet to fuck her way to the top!

Feeling better, she made dinner and they ate. Billy told her everything was set.

"I talked to Charlie. He's a good guy. You'll like him. He's here from New York for a week or so, staying at the Hilton. You go up, show him a good time. Get the money up front, of course."

She looked up. "How…How much should I charge?"

He smiled and she felt an uneasiness creep up on her. "Depends. For a fancy call girl, you could get five hundred or a thousand an hour…" he started to say.

"Th-that much?" It seemed like a fortune to her.

"Wait, I'm not done. With you, we have a unique opportunity."

She waited, watching him warily. What was he talking about?

"You look young, you see, even though you're legal. We can really use that."

Kristy's mouth dropped open. "You don't mean..."

"Yeah! Start your acting early! Pretend you're a fuckin' underaged virgin!"

"But that's illegal!"

He laughed and slapped his thigh. "You think any of this is legal? No, this is all just role playing, you know? You go, you pretend to be an innocent Valley girl or somethin', okay?"

"Valley girl? You mean like San Fernando Valley?"

"Yeah. Tell him you're sixteen. If you do, you could get two grand an hour, easy."

"Two..." She couldn't imagine that much money. All for having a little sex with some guy? It sounded too easy. Especially now that she was so horny. "And we split it, right?"

He snorted. "No, baby, you bring it all to me. I'll give you your cut, plus I'll let you stay here as long as you want."

"But...that's not fair!"

"Hey, I'm the one taking all the risks here! I set it up, I provide you protection, I give you food, clothes and a place to stay! If you can do better on your own, go for it!"

Because she couldn't do better right now, Kristy didn't press the issue. But she vowed to get away as soon as she could. She'd have to build up her own contacts, her own network of sugar daddies...

"Okay, clean this up and go take a shower—and shave that pussy. It's getting a little fuzzy. Put on some more of your new nice clothes."

She was startled from her reverie to realize this was really happening. At least this Charlie guy seemed nicer than Duane and his rough friends had been! That had been a real trial by fire! Fucking a nice New Yorker at the Hilton would be a cakewalk. Unless...

"Uh, Billy..."

"Yeah?"

"What will he expect? This Charlie?"

Billy smiled. "Oh, the usual stuff. A little role play, maybe some minor spanking—you know how it is with guys. They like to imagine they're the big bad he-man and you're the meek little girl who is overcome by his masculinity."

She nodded. She could do that, she supposed.

When she came out of the bathroom an hour later, she felt polished, primped and beautiful. She had on a pale yellow dress made of rayon that clung to every curve. It showed off her cleavage and came down to mid-thigh, making her look sexy without being slutty.

Billy whistled when he saw her. "Whoooie! You look like a million bucks!"

"Thanks." She twirled, feeling very much a woman now.

"Okay. It's after seven—go down and see Ronald, he'll take you to the Hilton. Charlie's in Room 415."

She nodded, feeling her stomach flutter. She was going out to be a high-priced call girl! To calm her nerves, she told herself she was an actress, playing a role. That's all this was. She put herself into the right frame of mind and imagined a director was about yell, "Action!"

"Okay. I'm ready."

"Good girl!"

Ronald also whistled when he saw her. "Oh, baby, you look fiiiine!" He twirled his forefinger, indicating she should turn around. She did, feeling flattered by all this attention. "Man! You are a hot one!"

"Thanks."

He stood there until Kristy lifted her dress to show off her panties. He grinned.

"All right, let's go. Don't want to keep the clients waiting."

She rode in the back and watched the streets drift by. She could spot homeless people, crowds of teenagers, wealthy people in limousines—a real melting pot of a city. She felt above them all, riding quietly in the Escalade like a woman in a dream.

Ronald pulled up in front of the hotel and turned to hand her a cell phone. "Here, baby, slip that into your purse and call me when you need a ride."

She thanked him as a valet rushed to open the door for her. She slipped out and smiled at him, still pretending she was on a movie set, with cameras behind her, shooting her entrance into the hotel. Walking with purpose in through the revolving door, she headed through the large atrium to the bank of elevators. The elevator had a glass front and she could see the people scurrying about, each with some important destination to attend.

The car stopped at the fourth floor and she got out. Kristy followed the signs to Room 415 and took a deep breath.

"Action," she whispered.

She knocked on the door. It opened at once and a rather ordinary-looking man in a dark suit open at the collar smiled at her. He looked like an insurance salesman, with his short brown hair and nervous eyes.

"Hi," he said. "You must be Kristy."

She nodded and made a note to herself to change her name if she was ever going to do anything like this ever again. She felt a wave of apprehension wash over her as she stepped past him. Her body felt hot and she wondered if she would be able to go through with this.

"Would you like a drink?"

"Uh, yeah."

He made her something and she took a big swallow, grimacing when the alcohol hit her stomach. She had no idea what it was but it seemed to help, so she took another swallow.

"I'm Charlie. You look really nice."

"Uh, you too," she said lamely.

"Billy really knows his girls—he tells me you're not even seventeen yet."

"Yeah. I'll be seventeen in a couple months though," she lied.

"And you're local? From the Valley?"

"Uh huh. I go to San Fernando High School," she said, hoping there was such a place.

"That's so…exciting. Do you have your driver's license yet?"

She shook her head. "No, not yet. My parents don't like me driving. They say I'm too immature."

"You don't look immature to me!" He stepped forward and his hands shook as he touched her bare shoulders. Kristy realized how easy this was going to be—he was more nervous than she was!

"How did you get away from them tonight?"

"Oh, I said I was staying at a girlfriend's house."

He nodded and his hands fumbled to touch her breasts through her dress. "You...like me?"

Suddenly, Kristy remembered to ask for the money up front. "Uh, sure. But I gotta get the money first, you know. I mean, I haven't done this kind of thing before..." That part was really true, she thought. Fucking Duane and his buddies seemed quite different from being an elegant call girl pretending to be underage.

"Sure, sure." He reached for his pants. She glanced down and saw his cock was already hard. "You're not a cop or anything are ya? I could get in a lot of trouble."

"No, I'm not a cop. Jeez, do I look like a cop? I mean, they don't hire kids, last time I checked."

He laughed. "Okay. Okay. Sure." He pulled out a wad of bills and started counting. Kristy just stared at the hundreds slipping by under his fingers. "It was a thousand an hour, right?"

She frowned. Had Billy worked out something different? "Uh...Billy told me it was two thousand an hour." He looked up sharply and she went on quickly, trying to play her part well. "I mean, I'm a virgin, you know. That's worth something."

His mouth dropped open. "Really?"

Kristy hoped she could pull that off. She remembered the blood when Billy had fucked her. "Yeah," she said. "I mean, I've fooled around with guys some. You know, kissing and petting."

Charlie nodded. "So I'll be your first?"

"Yeah. That was the deal."

"Why are you doing this? I mean, with a stranger and all."

"Oh, I need the money. And I figure, a girl's got something worth something, you know?" The more she talked, the easier it became to imagine herself as a young hooker. This was excellent training for a film role, she realized. She wished she had some gum to smack.

Charlie counted out several bills and handed them over. "This is gonna be so cool."

Kristy took the wad and began counting it. It was two hundred short. She looked up, her eyes narrow. "Hey! There's only eighteen hundred here!"

"Oh, sorry." He peeled off two more hundreds and handed them over. She smiled and put the wad into her small purse.

"Okay, now that that's out of the way, what would you like to do first?"

"Ohhh, I'd like to see you strip—slowly! Really sexy like!" He went and sat on the edge of the bed.

Kristy looked around. "Can I get some music?"

"Oh, sure!" He jumped up and turned on the clock radio. His fingers shook as he twirled the tuner until a sexy jazz tune came on. "How's that?"

She nodded. "That'll do." She bumped and grinded, swiveling her hips to the music and slipping the straps from her gown over her shoulders. Charlie's eyes were wide as golfballs and his mouth hung open. She felt more in control now and closed her eyes and played to the imaginary camera. Her dress fell to her hips and she heard him gasp. It didn't take much effort to push the silky material down until it fluttered to the rug. She stepped out of it and danced around in her bra and panties.

Coming close, she shook her breasts in his face. He buried his face in her cleavage and inhaled deeply. She laughed and spun away. Her hands went behind her back and unhooked her bra. She tossed it on the ground and turned to wiggle her tits at him. He leaned forward, his jaw working, his tongue licking his lips. Now her hands went to her hips and she realized, instinctively, that she was going too fast. So she slowed everything down and began to twirl around the room, coming close enough for him to reach out and touch her before spinning away again. She burned up ten minutes before her panties finally drifted to the floor.

It was like Charlie had gone into shock when he saw her shaved pussy. He leaned forward so far, he nearly fell over onto his face. "Oh god," he gasped, "oh my god."

"You like?"

"Oh yeah, baby!"

God, she thought, this was easy. The man was falling all over himself for her. She let go of her guilt and began to enjoy herself. She danced and wiggled and teased the man until she could see his erection straining against his pants. Kristy leaned forward and began unbuttoning his shirt. She thought Charlie might come in his pants! That would be funny—he'd be all done before he got started! Then she realized that would ruin everything—she had to make him last at least an hour! She slowed down. When he stood so she could unbuckle his pants, she accidentally touched his hard cock and he backed away and said, "Wait! Wait! Go slow!"

She laughed. "Want me to put my clothes back on for a while?"

"No, no. I just need a sec." He moved away and slipped off his pants. His boxer shorts were tented and Kristy watched as he went to the dresser and made himself another drink. He waved the bottle at Kristy, and she shook her head. She wanted to remain in control of her senses.

When he returned to her, he began running his hands over her naked body and she shivered with forced delight. She realized she was in a three-act play—and each act should last about twenty minutes. She glanced at the clock radio and noted barely fifteen minutes had passed. All right. More foreplay.

She danced away and Charlie watched her, his eyes bright. He nodded as she shook her young body and wiggled her hips, occasionally coming close to touch him before spinning away again. He slipped off his shorts and she saw his cock for the first time. It was nice, as cocks go, but no match to Leon's.

At last she moved closer and allowed him to capture her. He pushed her down onto the bed and began kissing her all over. She pretended to be shy and ticklish and virginal, all calculated to prolong the moment. She encouraged him to kiss her neck for several minutes before allowing him to kiss her breasts. Then she kept his attention on her breasts before she let him slip down to her pussy. It amazed her how easily she had fallen into her "role" as a hooker.

A hooker with a heart of gold, she thought to herself, smiling at the cliché.

Charlie spread her legs apart and began tonguing her pussy and Kristy began to forget her role and fought her inner demons. But it felt pretty damn good and she soon lost herself in the sensations. When she felt an orgasm building, it surprised her. How could she come with this stranger? What happened to her control?

She wrestled with herself for a few seconds before giving in and allowing the orgasm to swell within her.

"Oh! Oh my god! Oh Charlie!"

Encouraged, he redoubled his efforts and Kristy felt the bubble of her climax wash over her. "OH MY GOD!" Her body shook with the power of it. Charlie had a very talented tongue.

"Jesus, that was good!"

"Thanks. I'll bet you've never felt that before, huh?"

"Well, uh...No," she lied. "No guy ever did that!"

"That's the difference between boys and men," he told her, looking up from between her legs. "Boys you're used to dating are more interested in their own needs. Whereas men..." He shrugged. "We can be more patient and giving."

"I'll be sure and remember that!"

Charlie climbed up over her. "Now, I think you're ready."

"Wait! You need a condom!"

He looked disappointed. "Really? For two grand, I was hoping...."

"I could get pregnant! You don't want to have to support a kid, do you?"

"You mean you're not...?"

"No! My parents would kill me if I asked them if I could go on the pill!" Kristy fell right back into character.

"Oh, well...You got one?"

"Sure." She found her purse and pulled out a couple condoms. As she did, she glanced at the clock. Not quite a half-hour had passed. Things were going too quickly!

"But do we have to do it so soon?" she asked. "I mean, can we play around a bit first? It's all so new to me, you know."

"Oh, sure, sure!" he nodded. "Are you nervous?"

"Yeah. Will it hurt?"

"Oh, no, not the way I do it." His caring expression seemed a bit forced and Kristy pretended not to notice. Men are so transparent! All he cared about right now was sticking his cock in.

They cuddled together and he ran his hands all over her body. She let him have his way and he seemed to spend a lot of time teasing her pussy. It began to have the desired effect. Kristy soon forgot about her efforts to prolong the moment and started thinking about how nice it would be to have his cock inside her.

He moved up over her and she watched with lidded eyes as he fumbled to slip the condom over his cock. The condom was red and it gave his erection a pink glow. She smiled and spread her legs.

"Now, don't worry—I'll be gentle," he told her.

She nodded and tried to hide her impatience. When she felt the tip slip inside, it took all of her will power to keep her from grabbing his ass with both hands and pulling him hard. She tried to remember she was an innocent virgin who knew nothing and waited for him to ease more of his cock into her.

Her hips began to jerk with impatience and his cock went in further. He frowned and Kristy realized he was waiting to feel some resistance—and he would not!

"Ouch!" she said at once and he pulled back.

"Did I hurt you?"

"No, it was just a pinch," she said. "I was just startled, that's all."

"Okay. Let's try this another way." Suddenly, he shoved himself inside her and she gasped with the shock of it.

"Oh! Oh my god!" She cried out.

"Was that better?" he gasped, even as he started to thrust back and forth.

"No, I mean yes. It hurt for a sec—oh! Oh!" Her mind seemed to go away as his pounded her. Her role and her body merged into one as she felt his hard cock slide in and out. She squeezed at him with her vaginal muscles and she felt him erupt inside her.

"Uhhhhh!" he groaned and sank down on top of her.

Dammit, she thought—*it was too soon!* She hadn't come and she had wanted to prolong the moment. She continued to thrust her hips and that convinced Charlie to keep trying to force his softening cock inside her. She could see it was a losing battle, so she pretended to climax and sank down into the sheets.

"Wow!" he gasped. "That was great!"

"Really? I did okay?"

"Oh yeah baby, you're a great lover!"

He started to get up and Kristy held him in place and told him she wanted to "cuddle" because she was feeling a little bad about giving up her virginity. Charlie nodded sympathetically and lay with her for a while, telling her what a good girl she was and that she shouldn't feel bad.

When at last he pulled away and got up to remove his condom, she glanced at the clock to see she was still about ten minutes short. "Hey, can I have another drink? I need to calm my nerves."

"Oh, of course!" He made one quickly and handed it to her. She took a swallow and tried to slow everything down. She wasn't sure of the protocol now—did it matter if she didn't quite make it to a full hour? Would he ask her to refund a couple hundred dollars?

She needn't have worried. Charlie sat naked on the bed, sipping his drink and touching her body and talked about inconsequential things. She told him what subjects she liked in school, trying to remember what she was taking when she was a sophomore. Not that it mattered—she probably could've told him anything! He was far more interested in touching her for a few minutes before it was time to go.

She rose and got dressed. He watched, his eyes a bit sad as she pulled on her clothes.

"That was really nice," he told her. "Can I see you again?"

"Sure. Maybe. We'll see."

"I come into town often. I'll call Billy next time and ask for you, okay?"

"Okay." She remembered Billy had hinted that Charlie was some kind of producer and she asked, "Are you in the movie business?"

He tipped his head. "Why do you ask?"

"Oh, I'm hoping to be an actress someday, you know, so I just wondered."

"No," he said. "I'm a financial manager. But I have some stars as clients."

Kristy hid her disappointment. "Oh, that's interesting." She glanced at the clock. "Well, I'd better go."

"Thanks for a wonderful time."

She gave him a peck on the cheek and left. She called Ronald on the way to the elevator and he met her outside the hotel in the SUV. She got in and he turned and asked, "How did it go?"

"Pretty well, I think."

"You get paid?"

"Yeah."

He smiled and said, "Great. Billy will be pleased."

He drove them home and she went up to the apartment. Billy greeted her at the door.

"Well?"

"Charlie was nice."

"How much did you get?"

"Two thousand, like you said." Suddenly, she cursed herself for not lying and telling him it was only a thousand!

"Good, give it to me."

"I get half, right?" She knew it was a losing argument, but she felt she had to try.

He grabbed it out of her hand and pulled the wad out. "No, you get what I say you get." He counted it and nodded.

"That's not fair! I did all the work!"

"All you did was lay back and spread your legs. I set it all up!"

"I need some money! I can't work for clothes all the time!"

"You got a nice place to stay! I kicked Heather out and you get her room. That's a sweet deal!"

"I won't stay if I don't get something! You can't keep it all!"

He peeled off three hundred. "Here. Now you've got some walking around money, okay?"

Three hundred? For all that work? "It's not enough."

His hand snaked out and slapped her across the face. "I'll tell you what's enough! You were making two hundred to fuck Duane and you thought it was a good deal!"

Kristy stepped back, her hand against her face. This was a side of Billy she had only seem glimpses of before. Now she knew she was in the presence of a dangerous man. He could really hurt her if he wanted to. She turned at once and went down the hall to Heather's room. It was empty of all traces of her former friend. Kristy went to the closet and found all her clothes, including the new outfits, were hanging there. So it really was her room now. She wondered where Heather wound up.

She sat on the bed and thought about what she should do. Running away with just three hundred wasn't going to work. She had to figure out a way to conceal some more money from Billy! She could start lying about her earnings—but how to keep him from searching her purse—or her bra? There must be some way, she decided.

CHAPTER THIRTEEN

That night represented a change in Kristy's life, far more so than after she had gone out to "be nice" to Duane and his friends. It was as if Duane had been a warm-up and Charlie had represented her first day on the job.

The next morning, when Kristy woke up, enjoying her new bed and thinking about acting jobs, she was brought back to reality when she came out to get some coffee. Billy was already up.

"Hey, baby," he said before she could reach the kitchen. "I've got another job for you today."

"What?" She had planned to check out some audition possibilities.

"There's a new guy at the Biltmore. He loves the young virgin shit. He's expecting you at noon."

"What? No way—I've got to go see about acting jobs!"

He rushed forward and grabbed her with both hands, his fingers digging into her upper arms. "Listen, baby, you work for me now, you got it?"

"No! I don't want to work for you! This was just temporary!"

He slapped her and she stumbled to her knees.

"You work for me until I tell you you can go!"

"No! You can't! I'm an actress!"

He laughed, a cruel sound to Kristy's ears. "No, you're just another whore in Hollywood. You think a producer would want you now? It's already all over town that you're a girl who puts out."

She looked up, horrified. "What? What are you saying?"

"Duane and Charlie work for me, in a way. They break in new girls and spread the word. Now a lot of clients are lining up to get a crack at the new pussy."

Her mouth dropped open and tears came to her eyes. "Nooo."

"It's true. No one would hire you as an actress now. You're just another cute pussy. Now get cleaned up and go do what I tell ya."

"But...but...I can't! I came to Hollywood to be an actress! You know that! That's all I wanted to do! All this crap..." She waved her hands around, "was just to keep me from being out on the streets! Just until I could save up some money! You can't do this to me!"

"Sure I can. That's what I do. Now go get ready."

"No!" She stood up defiantly, not caring that Billy was a lot bigger and stronger than she was. It turned out to be a mistake. He slapped her again and when she went down, he pushed her over onto her stomach and slipped his belt from his pants.

She screamed and struggled but he was too strong. He ripped off her robe and began whipping her bare bottom with his belt. She cried and begged and tried to escape. When he stopped, she was a mess of tears and bruised flesh.

As she lay sobbing, he leaned down and said softly, "Now you gotta go out and work with your ass bright red. Your customers are gonna love it too 'cause they'll think you get off on that shit. So they'll beat you more, make you beg them to be allowed to suck their cocks and fuck them silly. And you'll do it. 'Cause if you don't, you'll get more of the same here."

"I won't, I won't," she sobbed. "You can't make me."

"Sure I can. As long as you do what you're told, you'll be well taken care of. I'll feed you and give you a nice place to live and some walkin' around money. But if you think you can just refuse to work, well, don't try it. Lot of girls did and they all regretted it."

"I'll run away, I'll go to the cops."

He laughed. "Yeah? Run away to where? Back home? And if you go to the cops, I'll make sure you're arrested for prostitution. Good luck gettin' an acting job with that on your record."

Kristy felt trapped and knew Billy had played her just right. She couldn't risk having an arrest record! And she couldn't go home, either. So she was faced with doing what Billy wanted or running away to find a new place to crash. That thought terrified her. It would be like starting over. And she had just three hundred bucks to her name. How long would that last?

Her only hope, she thought, was to keep her eyes open and make her break as soon as she could find a way. There must be someone who could help her!

"Now, what's it gonna be?"

For now, she thought, *I'll have to pretend to go along.* "I'll... I'll do it."

"Good girl. Get cleaned up and go down to Ronald's place around eleven-thirty. He'll take you."

She stood up and headed down the hallway on shaky legs.

"Oh, and Kristy?"

She turned. "Yeah?"

He flashed her a wolfish grin. "Wear something sexy."

She went to the bathroom to shower.

When she came out an hour later, she knew she looked good. She didn't dare try to defy him further—her ass was already sore enough. But she was determined to start hiding money from him. How? Would Ronald help? No, she couldn't trust him. Maybe she could hide the money somewhere and come back for it later. That idea had some possibilities. If worse came to worse, she could always hide a few small bills in her vagina. She shivered at the thought.

"Good. You look hot. Now Steve—that's the client—is expecting an underaged girl, so do your virgin routine like you did with Charlie. Ask for two grand, like before. We'll run this play as long as we can before you'll start looking too old to pull it off."

Kristy didn't see how that was possible—she was not even nineteen yet. She *was* still a kid! But she didn't argue. She meekly went downstairs and found Ronald and he took her to the Biltmore—after he made her flash him, of course. As she stood there in the hall, her dress held up, she felt like nothing but a tawdry whore.

"Room nine-oh-six," he told her after they pulled up, handing her the cell phone. She nodded and got out. There was no use trying to appeal to Ronald's better nature. He seemed just as greedy as Billy did.

She went upstairs and knocked on the door. It surprised her that she didn't feel as nervous about fucking another stranger. She was more concerned about building up an escape fund. The door opened and a tall man with hard eyes stared back. When he saw her, his face broke into a grin, but the eyes remained cold. Kristy stepped inside, her stomach lurching.

"Hi, you must be Kristy," he said.

Dammit—she had forgotten to tell Billy she wanted to change her name. "Yeah. You're Steve, right?" She looked around. They were in a very nice suite, roomy and expensive. She thought, *This man is rich!*

He nodded. "Take off your clothes."

Just like that, huh? She started to obey and stopped. "Uh, you need to pay me first. Billy said two thousand."

He stared at her for a long moment. "That's too much. I can tell right away you're no virgin. Who are you trying to kid?"

Her mouth opened and closed as she tried to think of some indignant response. "But...I mean...Yes, I'm a virgin! I'm only doing this because I need the mon—"

He slapped her across the face before she could finish. She staggered back and then turned and ran for the door. He grabbed her and tossed her onto the bed as if she was some kind of rag doll. This man was strong!

Kristy bounced and tried to roll off of it but the man was on her, tearing her dress and slapping at her hands when she tried to fight him.

"I like a girl with some fight in her," he said. "Turns me on."

She didn't know if it was better to fight or to go limp. But she didn't want to be raped, not without being paid first! "Wait! Wait!"

He paused.

"How about fifteen hundred?"

He laughed. "Doesn't look like you're in any position to bargain." He pulled her bra aside, exposing her breasts and pinched one of her nipples.

"Billy will be really mad if you don't pay me."

That seemed to stop him. He finally let her go and stood up. "Okay, okay. Fifteen hundred." He pulled a wad from his pants and counted out the hundreds and tossed them onto her chest. She gathered them up quickly and stuffed them into her purse. In that moment, Kristy understood why whores needed pimps.

She tried to get back into her "virgin girl" character but it proved to be impossible. Besides, he didn't believe it. "So what do you want, honey?" she tried to say as sweetly as she could.

He laughed. "I want to see you naked, for starters."

She rolled to her feet and stripped off her dress. Fortunately, it hadn't been ripped beyond repair. Her bra and panties came next until she stood naked and defiant in front of him. His eyes narrowed and he walked around her until he spotted her ass, still red from Billy's whipping.

"Ohhh, looks like you enjoy the hard stuff, huh?"

"No! That was...that was a mistake."

"I love to spank a pretty young thing. C'm here."

"No! I'm too sore!"

"I won't hurt you too much. I'll just use my hand. But if you'd like to fight, that's fine with me!"

He grabbed her and took her down over his knee. He began to spank her and it really hurt! She cried and begged and pleaded with him. Finally, he stopped and asked, "You gonna do what I tell you to do?"

"Yes! Yes! I promise!"

"Good." He dumped her onto the rug and unzipped his pants. "Let's start with this, huh?"

She dove on his hard cock, determined to bring him off quickly so she could escape this crazy man. But no matter how hard she tried, he refused to come! When her jaw tired, he pushed her away.

"Thanks. That was a good warm-up. Now bend over and put your face on the rug."

She obeyed and felt his hand on her back. Suddenly she remembered. "Wait! You have to wear a condom!"

"Hell no, I don't. Not for fifteen hundred!" And his cock was thrust into her all at once.

Kristy screamed, more out of shock than pain or fear. She couldn't really get pregnant, she tried to tell herself, but her mind couldn't concentrate while Steve was fucking her so mercilessly. She could only hang on and hope it would be over quickly.

It didn't take long. She felt him spasm and his hot seed erupted inside her. She was glad it was over so quickly. She didn't care if he didn't use up the entire hour. He stayed inside her for a long time before pulling out. She started to rise and he barked. "Did I tell you to get up?"

"Uh...no, but I thought..."

"Whores aren't paid to think. They're paid to fuck. And I'm not done yet."

She stayed there and waited for instructions.

"Okay boys, you can come out now!"

Kristy gasped and tried to rise again. But Steve was ready and slapped her bottom and she stopped resisting. She craned her head around to see two men emerge from the other room. They seemed rough, like Steve: One was medium-sized and bald, but very muscular, the other was taller with dark hair and wire-rimmed glasses, but his eyes were cold like Steve's.

"NO! I didn't agree to this! It was just supposed to be one!"

Another few slaps rained down on her ass. She cried out and bit her lip. "I paid for an hour—I expect to get an hour!"

"They'll have to pay me too!" She said, remembering Duane's friends.

"Hell I do. You agreed to fuck for an hour and that's what you'll do. Come on, boys, time's awastin'."

They laughed and bald head got to her first. She tried to fight him off but he, like Steve, apparently enjoyed a feisty woman. He grabbed her by the hips and even as she struggled, he easily managed to hold her while unbuckling his pants. The other two men hooted and cheered him on.

When she felt his hard cock spear into her, Kristy gave up and let him have her. Like Steve, he didn't use a condom. He fucked her hard and she lay with her head on the rug, afraid to move. She expected him to come but he didn't. Instead, he simply pulled out after a few minutes and made way for the second stranger.

He wanted her to roll over onto her back and pushed her roughly. The fight was just about all gone out of her and she put up just a token resistance. That earned her a slap across her breasts and she cried out.

"Whooo! Benny, you animal!" Baldy shouted, his hard cock still bobbing in front of him.

Benny slipped his cock inside her and began to fuck. Kristy lay back and let it happen. She felt a presence next to her and saw Baldy's cock bounce against her cheek.

"Suck it or you'll get my belt," he growled. She opened her mouth and took him inside.

When she felt Benny come, Baldy switched places with him and she was made to clean Benny's cock while Baldy fucked her again. When he finally came, Steve had gotten hard again and he fucked her.

When the hour was up, Kristy lay exhausted on the rug, her clothes scattered around her. The men went to the wetbar and poured themselves a drink. They didn't offer her one. She rolled over and struggled to her feet, feeling every ache and pain. She slowly got dressed as the men talked among themselves and watched her.

She knew Billy would be pissed that these men didn't pay. "I'm gonna tell Billy about this," she said, trying to sound threatening. "You guys had no right to triple up."

"She's right," Steve said to the two men. "How about giving the poor working girl a tip?"

The men laughed and came forward. Each handed her a one-hundred-dollar bill. She cursed them and grabbed her purse and fled. No one stopped her. She called Ronald with tears in her eyes, holding her ruined dress together with the other hand. In the elevator, she rolled up the two hundred dollars in tips and slid it into her sore vagina, wincing at the pain. When the big man pulled up, she hoped he would go upstairs and beat them up. He just shrugged and said, "Tell Billy." Just like that. He didn't seem to care that she was gang-raped!

Billy's reaction was quite different. "They paid you *what?*"

"Yeah! Steve said he didn't believe I was a virgin! I thought he was going to rape me for nothing, so I asked for fifteen hundred and he agreed! I was lucky to get that! And then he brought in these other two guys and they didn't pay me anything!" She dissolved into sobs.

He slapped her across the face, shocking her out of her self-pity. "Give me the money."

She handed him her purse and he counted out the bills. "That's all?"

"Yeah!"

"You didn't keep nothin'?"

"No! I told you!"

He grabbed her and threw her down on the couch. She screamed and tried to get away but it was useless. She felt him dig his fingers up between her legs and she felt a stab of fear that gave her new energy to fight him. He slapped her again and she sagged down, defeated. She felt his fingers discover her hidden cache and he pulled them out triumphantly.

"Ha! Holdin' out on me, are ya?"

He rolled her over onto her back and ripped her dress from her. She heard the sound of his belt slipping from his pants and began to beg.

"Please! That was just a tip! That was all they gave me! I worked hard! I earned it!"

Whack! Whack! Whack! The belt fell against her sore bottom and she cried and screamed. When he stopped and asked, "Are you gonna hold out on me again?" she babbled, "No, no, no!"

"Good." He stood up and put his belt back through the loops. "Now get cleaned up. You got another customer at five."

"No! I can't! I'm all beat up!"

"I don't care—that was your doing! Your job is to fuck and so you fuck where and when I say. And you bring me ALL the money, this time, you hear?"

"I can't, I can't," she sobbed. She despaired at every getting away from him.

His mood changed at once. He bent down and took his face into his hands and said softly, "Hey, I'm sorry. I know Steve can be rough at times. And I'm gonna talk to him about this, you hear? I'll make sure he understands how I want my girls to be treated, okay?"

She found herself nodding, desperate for a little sympathy and consideration.

"Now this next guy, he's really nice. He's more like Charlie. You liked Charlie, didn't you?"

"Yeah, Charlie was nice."

"Good. So just think of this as an easy job."

"What does this guy want?" She asked, not even realizing how she had already capitulated. "Does he want a virgin?"

Billy chuckled. "I don't think you look much like a virgin today. Let's just go with a 'young girl trying to make money to survive in this town' theme, okay?"

"How—how much should I charge?"

"Try for fifteen hundred. But with your bruises, if he bargains for twelve, take it. Just bring me back all the money, okay?"

She nodded and wiped away her tears.

"Good girl. Now go get cleaned up and take a nap or something. I'll wake you when it's time to go."

Kristy got up and padded obediently down the hall to take another shower. When she went into her room later, she checked to see it was already three-thirty. She lay down on the twin bed naked and tried to get some sleep but her mind wouldn't let her. Her dreams had been shattered and there didn't seem to be anything she could do about it.

CHAPTER FOURTEEN

Over the next three months, Kristy found it was better to just do what she was told to avoid Billy's wrath. When she did, he was nice to her, which she craved. He would hold her and tell her he loved her and make her feel like she mattered.

At first, she had been on the hotel circuit, which was mostly easy work. She encountered the occasional jerks like Steve, but most were nice to her. The "virgin whore" gambit faded away quickly, however, as few men were fooled by it and often became angry they were being cheated. Unfortunately, that meant she could no longer demand a premium price. Her regular price dropped to twelve hundred and occasionally it dipped to seven or eight hundred an hour, which always made Billy mad.

"That's the best you could do?" he'd demand. "You sure you're not holding out on me?"

"Search me!" She'd say. "He told me I wasn't worth twelve hundred and he was about to kick me out! What was I supposed to do, just walk away? Seven hundred was the best I could do!"

Kristy always felt under pressure to bring Billy as much money as she could. She gave up trying to keep any money for herself—it was just too risky. She feared him too much. He'd slip her a couple hundred here and there and she saved it as best she could, but it never seemed to be enough to allow her to break free of Billy's grip.

Her world was isolated between Billy, Ronald and the clients. She never saw Heather. So when she woke up one morning around eleven and came out for coffee, she was surprised to see her in the living room, talking to Billy.

"Hi, Heather," she said, not sure if she should hug her or curse her out.

"Hi, Kristy. Your hair looks, uh, good."

Kristy shrugged. She knew she didn't look good, hair or otherwise—she looked worn out and abused, but she didn't argue the point.

"I brought Heather here to help show you the ropes."

Kristy frowned. "I know the ropes."

"Not on the street, you don't."

Her heart seemed to stop in her chest. "What?"

"Heather will take you out tonight. You'll work her corner for now."

She fought her panic. "I'm not going out on the streets! I work the hotels, remember! I get good money for you!"

Billy shook his head. "Not anymore. You don't have that fresh-faced look that men like. Now you just look like another whore."

"Noo," she begged but she knew there was no use. "Please! I'll do better! I'll work harder! Give me a chance!"

"Sorry. That's how it goes in this business. Girls start out looking like, well, like you did—fresh off the farm. But after a few short months, they take on that hollow look you have now. And men in the hotels want the fantasy. They'll pay for the fantasy, you know. You no longer can convince them you're a sweet, innocent girl."

Kristy began to cry and Heather tried to comfort her but she shoved her arms away. Heather shrugged and stepped back.

She begged and cried some more, but it was no use. Billy had made up his mind. She was now a streetwalker.

"It's too bad you didn't let us take nekkid photos," he pointed out. "If you had, you would've had light duty for months. Some of those girls earn really good money, too. But you wanted to keep your face and body pure, so you chose to become a whore. And in this town, whores get old fast."

That evening around seven, as she and Heather were ready to go out, he told her she had to charge what everyone else charged, which was one-fifty for a blowjob or three hundred for a fuck. It sounded like peanuts to Kristy, whose last job had earned her seven hundred.

"Your quota tonight is just twelve hundred," he told her. "I'm giving you a break. Heather will watch out for you, okay?"

"Quota?"

"Yeah. That's how much I expect, minimum. You don't want to know what happens if you fail." His hand went to his belt and Kristy knew exactly what he meant. Her ass had barely healed from her last whipping, four days ago.

"How-how much is Heather's quota?" She wanted to know what she'd have to bring in later.

"What are you up to now, Heather?"

The girl grimaced. "Twenty-two hundred."

"That's my girl. Oh, Kristy, you'll need this." He handed her a key to the apartment door. She stared at it like it was the Holy Grail.

"Now off with you two. Don't come back until you've earned your money."

As they rode the elevator, Kristy asked, "Why can't we keep some money?"

Heather shrugged. "That's how he keeps us close to him. We need him to survive. If we made a ton of dough, we'd all leave as soon as we could."

"It's so wrong!"

"I know, but there it is."

Ronald drove them downtown. Heather's corner was off Melrose, a popular street, although they were far from the trendy shops. This corner seemed a bit too seedy for Kristy's comfort and she got out nervously, staying close to Heather.

"Now, here are the rules," she said. "Ronald is going to park right up the block. The deal is, when a car stops, first thing we do is, memorize their plate. Ronald will do that too, but it's a good habit to get into in case something goes wrong."

Kristy shivered but said nothing.

Heather continued, "Then we ask them what they want. They'll ask how much for this or that. Remember our prices. You can go lower if you wanna, like when you're short on your quota and time's running out, but I wouldn't do it early in the evening. When you guys agree, you wave to Ronald so he and the customer both know you got your pimp right here and that usually stops any funny business. You get in and have him drive to that lot down the block. We do most of our business there. It's close enough so if you scream, Ronald will be right there. He doesn't always stay, but he will tonight."

"Jesus, Heather, you do this every night? How can you stand it?" She didn't think she could make it.

Heather seemed to delight in Kristy's fear. "Just relax. It's easier than you think. We girls were made to fuck, you know. And by now, I'm sure you know how to use that pretty mouth of yours." She grinned. "Okay, where was I? Oh, yeah. You get your money up front, same as always. You do the job and you walk back here—don't let him drive you! He may take off on ya and you'll wind up who knows where."

"Oh, god, Heather, you're scaring the shit outta me!"

"Take it one client at a time. Most are real nice. They just want to get their rocks off. They'll pay you, you suck or fuck and you're back here before you know it. You give Ronald your money so no one can rob you."

And that was it. Heather said she'd give Kristy the first drive-by and the younger girl stood by the curb, trying to look alluring in her mini-skirt and leopard-print top. It was a bit chilly out there and she hoped she wouldn't freeze to death before she earned her "quota." That concept sounded so barbaric!

A man pulled up at once and Kristy was so flustered she forgot to memorize the license plate number. She went to the window and it rolled down so she could stick her head in.

"Hi," she said nervously. "You want a date?"

"How much for a BJ?"

"Uh, one-fifty."

"Shit! That much? How about you do me for seventy-five?"

"No, that's not enough."

"One hundred?"

Kristy looked around at Heather. The older hooker gave her a sharp look as if to say, *Stick to your guns.*

"No. One-fifty is the right price for this fine mouth," she told the man.

He shook his head and drove off in a huff. Kristy barely got her head out of the window in time. She turned and said to Heather, "I gave up an easy hundred!"

Heather laughed. "Don't fall for those cheapskates. You're worth more 'cause you're new."

Heather grabbed the next car that pulled up. She talked too softly for Kristy to hear, but she must've come to an agreement because she jumped in and the car sped off. While

Heather was gone, another car came by and cruised to a stop. This time, Kristy remembered the license plate.

"Hey, I haven't seen you around here before. You new?"

"Yes I am and I'm good." She winked at him.

"What's your name?"

She thought fast. She didn't want to use her real name out here. "Crystal," she said, using the first name that came to mind.

Kristy convinced the man to pay one-fifty for a BJ by pulling down the top of her tank top to show him the swell of her breast.

"Hop in," he said. He was a scrawny man about forty and he looked harmless enough. She waved to Ronald and jumped in. She directed him around the corner to the parking lot and he parked and eased his seat back.

"Go for it."

"Uh, you gotta pay me first."

"No I don't. You suck first, then I pay. That's how it's done."

"Bullshit. You want to talk to my pimp about it?" She pulled out her cell phone.

"Whoa! No, no need for that." He dug into his pocket and found a dirty wad of bills. "Here." He seemed disgruntled.

Kristy counted out the money and slipped it into her purse. She bent down and unzipped him, hoping this would go fast. She had a lot of work to do tonight! For several minutes, she shut off her brain and just let her mouth pleasure his cock until he squirted. She pulled back and smiled at him as she swallowed, grimacing a bit at the sour taste, and zipped him up.

"Thanks," he said. "Maybe I'll see you again sometime."

She got out and walked back to the corner. Heather was there.

"How did it go?"

Kristy shrugged. "I did my first BJ. It was okay." She tried to act nonchalant about it, but she wished she were somewhere else.

It took Kristy until nearly midnight to reach her quota. She had given mostly blowjobs, but a few men had wanted to fuck her. It wasn't easy to maneuver in the backs of some of their vehicles and she realized it would be a lot easier for the men if she were nothing but a pussy and a torso—no limbs and no head. She huddled in the car with Ronald after she was done, watching Heather work the cars by herself for the last hour and a half until she made her quota.

When they finally got home, it was almost two a.m. Everybody was too tired to talk. Heather was dropped off at a small apartment building a couple blocks from Billy's place and waved as she went inside. She didn't seem to be upset that Kristy had replaced her in Billy's apartment.

Kristy trudged up to Billy's place and used her key to let herself in. She went directly to bed, stopping only long enough to brush her teeth and gargle with mouthwash. She fell into a dreamless sleep.

She woke at noon and came out to see Billy up and around. He'd already had his coffee and he let her pour herself a cup before he asked about her night.

"It was awful," she said.

He didn't seem to care. "Did you make you quota?"

"Yeah." She found her purse and handed over the thirteen hundred she had earned, one hundred more than the minimum he had set.

He gave her a big grin and a hug. "I'm proud of you, sweetheart."

"I'd like to keep some, Billy," she whined.

He peeled off a hundred. "I'm a softie when it comes to pretty faces." He winked. "Now how about giving your old boyfriend a blowjob—let me see how much you've learned."

Kristy knew better than to object. Yes, he had given her a hundred dollars, but now she was about to earn it. She did her duty quickly and was rewarded with a tongue bath. He patted her head. "That's my girl."

EPILOGUE

Crystal sat on the bus bench, looking through the crowd. It was a sunny day in early June, a perfect time to find new talent for Billy. Schools were out and girls were heading to California to become starlets. She shook her head. What a bunch of saps!

It had been two years since she had arrived, eager and breathless, certain she would be discovered and make millions in films. It took just about three months for those dreams to be shattered. It had been hard, at first, to make the transition. She kept thinking of herself as a budding actress who occasionally hooked to make ends meet. Under Billy's relentless pressure to earn more, she soon forgot her dreams and just concentrated on surviving each night.

Her quota had risen to more than two thousand a night, forcing her to work harder and longer to keep Billy happy. One night, after she had failed and been beaten, she had been sent to live with the others in the crib and told she could come back when she earned her quota regularly.

Heather had been among the girls at the crib, which was a three-bedroom apartment. The girls slept two to a room. The place was always messy, as some of the girls hated to clean up after themselves and the others refused to be their maids. Kristy despised it and vowed to return to Billy's favor as soon as she could. She knew it was his way of making his girls work harder.

She had a dream to escape that lasted about a year. She kept squirreling away money here and there until she had saved up a fifteen hundred dollars and kept it hidden under her mattress. Then she came home one night to add a meager one hundred to her stash and discovered it was missing. She raised holy hell, but every girl swore up and down they hadn't taken it. She told Billy and his only response was: "You been holdin' out on me, girl?"

She had been crushed and something inside her died that day. From then on, she went through the motions, fucking and blowing strangers and handing the money over to Billy. She kept only a couple hundred aside for herself. Less for others to steal.

It was a few months later that Heather vanished. She had gone out one afternoon to run errands and never came back. Crystal thought she had been saving up and had finally managed to escape, but it seemed odd that she hadn't told anyone about it. Crystal was sure she would've send word to her somehow. But the weeks passed and nothing was heard. It was as if she had dropped off the face of the world. She asked Billy about it for several weeks, until he began to get testy and she dropped it. The one bright spot that came out of that was that Crystal was able to move back into Billy's apartment for a few weeks.

It was only recently that he made her his "bottom girl" and she was determined to live the good life as long as she could.

Crystal spotted a young girl with Asian features coming out from the bus from Phoenix. She knew the bus had originated in Alabama and had passed through dozens of towns on its way west. The girl was cute, standing maybe five-two, with dark short hair. She had a backpack slung over one shoulder and that wide-eyed look of the innocent. Crystal pushed herself up off the bench and approached her.

"Hi, you look a little lost. You waiting for someone?"

The girl's eyes narrowed as she eyed the friendly stranger. Up close, Crystal could tell she was half-Asian. "Uh, no. Why do you ask?" She had a lilting southern accent, Crystal noted. She pegged her from Alabama, Mississippi or Louisiana. Definitely east of Texas.

"Oh, I just saw you there and thought I could help. I live here, you see. I was waiting for my sister but she just called and said she missed the bus! Can I give you directions to a motel or something?"

"Well, I am looking for a cheap place to stay," the girl said.

Crystal laughed. "Well, there's cheap and nasty and decent and expensive—which did you have in mind?" She stuck out a hand. "I'm Crystal, by the way."

The girl took it. "I'm Sally. Sally Peterson."

"Where ya from, Sally?"

"Shreveport."

"What brings you out to our beautiful city?"

"I'm going to be an actress!"

"Well, good for you. If you want, I can show you around, help you find a place to stay."

"Oh, would you? That would be ever so nice of you!"

Together, the two headed out into the California sunshine, the bottom girl and the fresh-faced starlet.